THE SECRET OF PHANTOM ISLAND

Other Books
by Dustin Brady

Trapped in a Video Game

Trapped in a Video Game: The Invisible Invasion

Trapped in a Video Game: Robots Revolt

Trapped in a Video Game: Return to Doom Island

Trapped in a Video Game: The Final Boss

Superhero for a Day

Who Stole Mr. T?: Leila and Nugget Mystery #1

The Case with No Clues: Leila and Nugget Mystery #2

Bark at the Park: Leila and Nugget Mystery #3

THE SECRET OF PHANTOM ISLAND

DUSTIN BRADY

ILLUSTRATIONS BY JESSE BRADY

Andrews McMeel
PUBLISHING®

Escape from a Video Game: The Secret of Phantom Island
copyright © 2020 Dustin Brady. All rights reserved. Printed in the United
States of America. No part of this book may be used or reproduced in
any manner whatsoever without written permission except in the case
of reprints in the context of reviews.

Andrews McMeel Publishing
a division of Andrews McMeel Universal
1130 Walnut Street, Kansas City, Missouri 64106

www.andrewsmcmeel.com
I've hidden a message on pages 86–89.
Another clue will tell you how to decode the message.

20 21 22 23 24 RR4 10 9 8 7 6 5 4 3 2 1

ISBN Paperback: 978-1-5248-5880-3
ISBN Hardback: 978-1-5248-5887-2

Library of Congress Control Number: 2020937421

Made by:
LSC Communications US, LLC
Address and location of manufacturer:
2347 Kratzer Road
Harrisonburg, VA 22802
1st Printing—7/20/20

ATTENTION: SCHOOLS AND BUSINESSES

Andrews McMeel books are available at quantity discounts with bulk purchase
for educational, business, or sales promotional use. For information, please
e-mail the Andrews McMeel Publishing Special Sales Department:
specialsales@amuniversal.com.

Introduction

You know the deal with books by now, right? Left to right, top to bottom, keep turning pages until you see "The End." You've probably read so many books that you could write a book on reading books. (Please don't. It would be a very boring book.)

Well, this book is different. It's so different, in fact, that you probably need to read a book (or at least this introduction) to figure out how you should read it.

1. Only turn to pages you're instructed to in boxes that look like this:

SELECT

29 Grenade launcher.

20 Wingsuit.

If you read the book in order, you'll be confused and leave a devastating one-star review.

2. Choose wisely. Because this is a video game, wrong moves will often bring death. Just like a video game, though, death isn't permanent. Each death sends you back to a checkpoint where you'll get to try another decision.

RETURN TO CHECKPOINT ON P. 43

3. Some of the puzzles you'll find in this book are challenging. If you have trouble solving any of them, try slowing down and rereading the directions. Ask an adult for help. If you're totally stuck, turn to the back of the book for hints and solutions.

4. On your first read-through, focus only on beating the game while losing as few lives as possible. Don't go back to try different options, and don't worry about the secret letters associated with each ending.

5. Once you beat the game, go back and find every ending. Record the secret letters associated with each achievement in the back of the book to discover a code you can use to unlock a whole new story. Here's what the secret letters look like:

6. You can write in this book unless it's an e-book or library copy. In those cases, visit escapefromavideogame.com to print a worksheet to use instead.

You can make this book feel more like a video game by keeping track of your deaths. Each time you lose a life, return to the last checkpoint and cross a life off this page. If you lose all your lives, you must restart from the beginning.

CHOOSE GAME DIFFICULTY

EASY: INFINITE LIVES

MEDIUM: ♡ ♡ ♡ ♡ ♡ ♡ ♡ ♡ ♡ ♡

HARD: ♡ ♡ ♡ ♡ ♡

The Adventure Begins

CLOSE YOUR EYES and picture the greatest video game experience of your life. Maybe it came from a twist that turned your world upside down. Maybe a particularly beautiful level transported you somewhere you could never imagine on your own. Maybe you're thinking of a sequence so intense that it caused a full-body sweat.

Got that moment? Good. Now, open your eyes and understand this: that game is a pile of wet garbage compared to the wonder of *Cooper Hawke and the Secret of Phantom Island.*

Cooper Hawke and the Secret of Phantom Island could be the greatest video game in the history of video games. It's the third and final entry in the *Cooper Hawke* series, a series that has to date inspired seven professional video game journalists to weep actual tears of joy during their review.

What makes Cooper Hawke so great? First, he's a treasure hunter, which is such a cool job that it only exists in video games and cable TV. Also, Hawke pulls off feats like surfing on crocodiles, diving into erupting volcanoes, and defeating ancient forces of evil without breaking a sweat. Finally, and perhaps most importantly, his signature weapon is a grenade launcher.

Now, listen. Should a treasure hunter consider a signature weapon that's less likely to explode the very treasure he's hunting? Should he rethink even having a signature weapon in the first place, since treasure isn't known for fighting back? Should you stop asking lame questions? Grenade launchers are awesome, Cooper Hawke is awesome, and you'd probably be a lot more awesome yourself if you took a few minutes to chill out and launch some 'nades.

A perfect hero needs a perfect villain, and Cooper Hawke could not ask for a nastier nemesis than Declan Redgrave. In the previous game, Redgrave kidnapped Hawke's mom, stole his dog, and blew up his treasure collection with Hawke's own grenade launcher. And that was just in the first five minutes. *The Secret of Phantom Island* promises the final showdown between Hawke and Redgrave. There are rumors that the world's most advanced artificial intelligence engine is powering Redgrave for this game, so you know the confrontation is going to be intense. Think you're up for the challenge?

Unfortunately, you'll never find out. Neither will anyone else. That's because *Cooper Hawke and the Secret of Phantom Island* was being developed by Bionosoft, a video game company that got shut down by the U.S. government a month before the game's release because the CEO committed high crimes and misdemeanors. "High crimes and misdemeanors" is a boring lawyer phrase that usually refers to boring crimes such as "dereliction of duty." Not this time. This time, it means "trapping people in video games."

Bionosoft figured out how to put real people into real video games. There are about 10 million sweet things you can do with that discovery (over a million of which involve grenade launchers). Bionosoft didn't do any of them. Instead, they immediately hatched a plot that would doom the entire human race. Just before the company could launch their plan, they were stopped by a pair of 12-year-olds named Jesse Rigsby and Eric Conrad. Everyone was super grateful to Jesse and Eric for saving them, but also like 2 percent mad that this meant they'd never get to experience *Cooper Hawke and the Secret of Phantom Island* for themselves. (As *Game Guru* magazine put it, "Our tears of joy have turned to tears of anguish.")

It's been 11 months since the collapse of Bionosoft. In those 11 months, 1.2 billion new pictures of cute dogs have been uploaded to the internet. The world has been doing its very best to keep up with all those doggos, which hasn't left time for much else, especially remembering events that happened 11 whole months ago. As a result, almost everyone has already forgotten about *Cooper Hawke and the Secret of Phantom Island*.

You'd forgotten the game yourself until you spotted this book on the shelf two minutes ago. The title and cover both intrigued you, but what interested you more was the faint humming sound you heard.

Hmmmmmmmmmmmm.

When you pulled the book off the shelf, the humming grew louder.

HMMMMMMMMMMMM.

And now, while you're reading this, the humming is even louder still.

HMMMMMMMMMMMM.

Books don't usually hum, do they? That's because they don't contain the kind of technology this one does. You see, this book can finally bring you *Cooper Hawke and the Secret of Phantom Island*.

Really? How? Wait, what?! Don't worry about any of that. You've got 10 seconds to decide what to do.

10 . . . 9 . . . 8 . . .

SELECT

11 Let's do it!

171 No way, weird book!

HOW TO PLAY *Cooper Hawke and the Secret of Phantom Island*:

    1. Place your finger in the space below.

    2. Stare at your fingernail.

    3. You should notice the lines around your finger start to move. The technology is working. Continue staring for 10 seconds.

    4. Close your eyes and take a deep breath.

    5. Turn the page.

PLACE THUMB HERE

NNNNRROOOOOOOOOOOOOOM!

You feel something hard and plastic in your hand. It's a controller, just not a video game one. It's an airplane control wheel. This is unfortunate for a few reasons:

1. You don't know how to fly a plane.

2. This particular plane is burping black smoke and zooming toward the ground at 400 mph.

You realize too late that this book's introduction left out a small, yet (some might argue) important detail. It didn't bring you *Cooper Hawke and the Secret of Phantom Island*, it brought you INSIDE *Cooper Hawke and the Secret of Phantom Island*. You panic and yank on the control wheel. It flops in your hand.

"AHHH!" you scream.

Nnnrooooooooooo . . .

"AHHHHHHHHHH!"

OoooooooOOOOOOO . . .

"AHHHHHHHHHHHHHH . . ." (deep breath) ". . . AHHHH-HHHHHHHHHHHHHHH!"

On the third scream, something weird happens. The plane vibrates for a moment, then shatters into a million tiny pieces. You're still holding the control wheel, but now you're in a brightly lit cube of a room where each wall is composed of countless tiny mirrors. You're so shocked by this development that you stop mid-scream. Then, just as quickly as the plane blew apart, it reassembles itself.

NnnnrroooooooOOOOOOOM!

Wait, what was—are you in some sort of government experiment?! This is officially nightmare territory. "Weird book!" you yell. "I changed my mind! I wanna be done now!"

In response, two items lying on the copilot seat start glowing: Cooper Hawke's signature grenade launcher and a folded wingsuit. Which do you use?

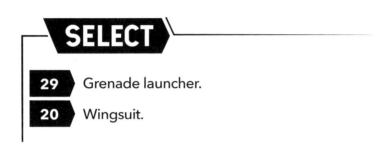

SELECT

29 Grenade launcher.

20 Wingsuit.

YOU TUG ON the lowest vine. Seems sturdy enough. You kick off the wall and . . .

THWIP!

The vine wraps around your wrist and yanks you up. You know why? Because it's a vine! You're being chased by vines! Why would you trust a vine on this island?!

The vine swings you back and forth a few times, then lets you go. You fly through the air, and another vine catches you. That vine tosses you to another vine, which tosses you to another vine, which tosses you to another vine. You finally stop struggling and let these vines have some fun. They gleefully toss you around the cave for a while longer, until the vine closest to the waterfall swings you up and over onto dry land. See, that wasn't so . . .

Uh-oh. Looks like the super-vine is waiting for you.

R ❗ ACHIEVEMENT UNLOCKED
NEVER TRUST A VINE
RETURN TO CHECKPOINT ON P. 43

THE VINE LUNGES FIRST. It yanks your leg just as you squeeze the trigger of your grenade launcher.

BOOM!

The grenade explodes when it hits the ceiling, which causes a cave-in in front of the wolf. One down, one to go! You load a second grenade while the vine drags you along the ground. You finally get the gun loaded and point it at the vine. But just before you can pull the trigger, a second wolf tears the weapon out of your hand. Then, the wolf catches your shirt. The vine tries pulling you away, but the wolf is good at this game. It's a winner-take-all round of tug-of-war, and you're the rope.

X ❗ ACHIEVEMENT UNLOCKED
YOU'RE THE ROPE
RETURN TO CHECKPOINT ON P. 43

YOU STAND ON the green section of the circle. Nothing happens. You bounce a little bit. Still nothing. Finally, you look to the sky. "What do you want me to dooooooooo . . ."

While you're looking up, a vine snatches your ankle and starts pulling you away.

"Hey!" You yank, but the vine has a vice grip. You keep squirming until the vine sprouts another stem that ties your wrists. "HEY!"

The vine drags you faster through the brush. You curl up to keep your face from getting smacked. Suddenly, the smacking stops. You sneak a peek to find that you're being lifted high enough to see the whole island. Then—*SMACK!*—back to more face-smacking, this time courtesy of branches at the top of the tree. The vine loops you in and out of more branches before tossing you onto solid ground.

You rub your eyes and look around. You're sitting in something that's the size and shape of a house, but it's completely covered in ivy, moss, and flowers. You walk to a nearby window and immediately feel dizzy. You're inside a tree house perched hundreds of feet in the air. Maybe there's a really long rope ladder in here? Nope. Just a Shandling page.

After you finish reading, you look for the carving Shandling mentioned and find it next to the front door.

May 23, 1975

Today, I discovered that my team and I are not the first inhabitants of Phantom Island. It has come to my attention that a sprawling village exists at the very top of the great tree.

Having explored the centuries-old village, I can say with confidence that it is a feat of engineering unlike anything on Earth. It is built at a height greater than today's skyscrapers, yet I cannot discern how its builders even arrived here in the first place, let alone carried their materials up the tree. The craftsmanship is so excellent and the attention to detail so precise that I suspect the entire village could survive a cyclone without losing a single plank.

It appears that my team needs to cross the village to accomplish our mission. It also appears that many dangers lurk in the treetop. I have lost several good men to this task already. I believe I have made a breakthrough, though. A carving in the first house appears to provide the details necessary to cross the village without casualty. Perhaps tomorrow will be the day that we succeed.

—William K. Shandling

Cooper Hawke trusts his mind, and so should you. Do your best to memorize this picture and complete this section without turning back to it.

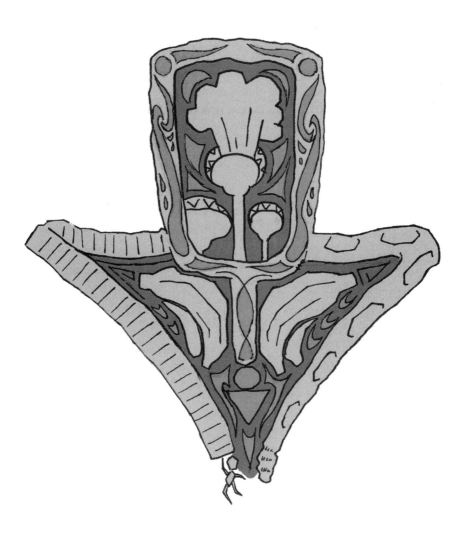

You take a mental snapshot of the carving, open the door, and gasp. There's a whole village of tree houses up here, all connected by rope bridges. You squint and spot something glowing green way off in the distance. That must be where you need to go.

You test the first rope bridge with one foot. Seems sturdy enough. You move your second foot onto the bridge and bounce a couple times. You've seen movies, so you know that these old jungle rope bridges always break. It's kind of their thing. But this bridge holds firm. You take a few more steps onto the bridge, then—*POW!*—a King Kong gorilla with orange eyes swings out of a tree and lands in the middle of the bridge.

The gorilla pounds his chest a few times, then stomps his feet. The bridge starts buckling in waves. You try to jump over the waves, but you don't have Cooper Hawke's leaping skills, so you're left to hang onto the rope and flop around. Next, the ape starts throwing bananas at you. Usually, a few bananas aren't a big deal, but these are bad bananas because they're covered in spikes. You run back and forth on the bridge to dodge them until the ape stops to rest.

You realize that the game is giving you a chance to strike, so you pull out your grenade launcher. Where do you shoot?

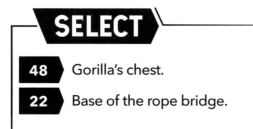

SELECT

48 Gorilla's chest.

22 Base of the rope bridge.

YOU UNFOLD ONE of those squirrel suits that people use to glide off of mountains in energy drink commercials. Once you put it on, you make the unfortunate discovery that it was made for Cooper Hawke's body, and you do not have Cooper Hawke's body. Not even close. You look like a toddler playing dress-up.

You stumble to the back of the plane and bang your shoulder into a mangled door. It flies off its hinges, and you're suddenly faced with a 20,000-foot fall. Gulp. You remind yourself that this is just a video game, then spread your arms and jump.

Flapflapflapflap.

This does not feel like a cool commercial. You're flopping and flapping like crazy, which only seems to make you fall faster. Finally, you grab the wings and yank them up like they're a pair of hand-me-downs.

Flapflap-whoooooosh!

You level out, take a breath, then search for your plane. There it is. Looks like someone had been using it for target practice. You watch the plane hit the ground and explode, then you look down and get a surprise.

Someone is driving a convertible below you and waving wildly. Who is that? The driver looks up, and you recognize her as Landra Lovato, Cooper's former treasure-hunting rival and current love interest. She seems to be motioning for you to glide into her back seat. Seriously? You're lucky that you figured out this wingsuit enough to avoid crashing on your face, and now you're supposed to steer? You grip the wings harder and do your best to follow the car along the winding road.

When you get close enough to hear Landra, she shouts, "Nice job, Coop! Now, bring it in!"

Her voice sounds a little different than you remember from previous games. They must have hired a new voice actor. You tuck your head and drift down. Your landing's not as smooth as the one Cooper Hawke would have pulled off—you kick Landra in the head—but you make it.

"Sorry!" you say. "I didn't mean . . ."

You stop when Landra turns around. She's grinning creepily. Then, she grabs her hair and pulls. It's a mask.

"Surprised?" It's Declan Redgrave. Before you can throw a punch, he shoots you with a tiny gun. Something stings your neck. You wobble for a second, then everything turns black.

TURN TO

P.36

ⓘ ACHIEVEMENT UNLOCKED
TERRIBLE RED BULL COMMERCIAL

YOU REMEMBER THE person swinging on the carving and re-alize there's a way you can do that yourself. You spin and shoot a grenade at your side of the bridge.

BOOM!

The gorilla looks confused, then horrified when he realizes what's going on. He scrambles away from you just as the bridge disconnects from your tree house. You hold on and swing to-ward the next branch.

THUNK!

The collision with the tree knocks the wind out of you and shakes the gorilla loose. He starts falling. You squeeze your eyes closed and prepare for an uncomfortable encounter with the backside of a giant monkey. But one millisecond before the gorilla smashes into you, you feel the bridge shake as he catches himself. You grab onto the gorilla's fur, and he carries you to the top of the bridge.

Success! You let go to continue your journey, but the goril-la's not done with you. He picks you up and throws you high into the tree. You land right in the middle of three more gorillas eating edenberries. They don't look happy.

"Hey guys," you try. "Didn't mean to interrupt family time. I just . . ."

The gorillas beat their chests and start chasing you.

"AHHH!" You run as fast as you can along the twisting branches, but stumble when the video game world briefly glitches. Everything gets blocky for just a moment, which causes you to lose your balance. You nearly tumble, but something invis-ible holds you up. Before you have time to wonder what just happened—*BOOM!*—one of the apes lands in front of you. You jump down to a lower branch, then use a giant leaf to bounce to the next branch.

PLOP! PLOP! PLOP!

The apes all land behind you and continue chasing. They're way faster than you because they've been eating edenberries, and since they're primates, they have just a bit more practice at this running-through-trees thing than you do. Last chance to do something.

On your right is a piece of bark that looks like it could be used to sled down a vine. On your left is a thin branch that ends in the biggest bunch of bananas you've ever seen. Where do you go?

SELECT

24 Sled.

70 Bananas.

YOU HOP ONTO the sled. When you woke up this morning, you did not imagine that one of your main activities would be sledding down giant vines, but here you are for the second time today. You hold tight through the jungle roller coaster as you zoom down inclines, pop over hills, and balance through loop the loops. Then, just as you allow yourself to relax and enjoy the ride, it's over. But instead of pulling into the station, this roller coaster spits you into something that resembles a trap. A bamboo door slams behind you. You shake it. It's locked.

Then, you hear a grunting noise above you. The gorilla from the bridge is smiling down at you. You realize too late that these superintelligent gorillas have figured out a new way to trap their dinner, and you're on the menu tonight.

R ❗ ACHIEVEMENT UNLOCKED
DINNER'S READY
RETURN TO CHECKPOINT ON P. 22

BACK IN THE CUBE, you search frantically for the right mirror. There must be thousands! How do you know which one is correct? Your clone watches your movements with a smile. It knows it can kill you whenever it wants. Finally, it pulls the berry back out.

"Sure you don't want this?"

That's when you spot it.

> *Find the mirror that is slightly off from the rest. Once you find it, put your thumb over the image and follow the instructions you received by humming the highest note you can. Hum for 10 seconds, then turn the page to find out if it worked.*

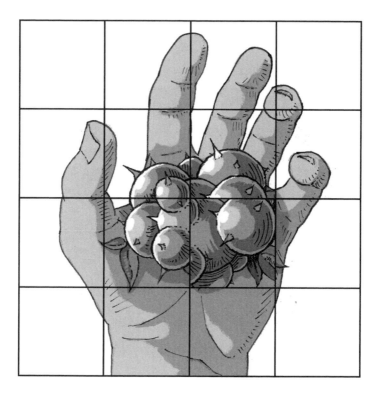

At first, the noise doesn't seem to do anything, but then you feel a vibration in your chest. You hum louder. Your clone looks concerned. The air itself seems to be vibrating now. You feel like it's hard for you to get air, but you don't want to let up, so you start screaming. That causes your clone to reach out, but its hand explodes into a million particles. The room does the same thing. It's just like your very first moments in the video game when you screamed and everything blew apart!

This is all very encouraging, but you don't want to let up. You dig deep and scream as loud as you can until you're standing in darkness. You only stop screaming when you feel a book in front of your face.

You take a deep breath. You're out. You won.

The book doesn't seem to be humming anymore. You carefully reopen it. All its pages are blank. Was any of that real? You decide not to bring it up with anyone you know because you'd like to keep your reputation as a non-crazy person. Instead, you take a moment to enjoy the real world, where there's an almost zero chance of getting chased by killer bees. Then, you go home, throw this book into a trash bag, throw that trash bag into another trash bag, then throw the whole thing into a third trash bag, which you double knot and bury deep in your closet.

Then, you open a computer and start investigating. You can't find anything online for "edenberry." Same thing for "William K. Shandling," "Bionosoft artificial intelligence project," or "secret island with deadly tree." You're just about to close your computer and go to bed when you hear a *DING*.

You have a message, which is weird because you didn't have any messaging apps open. A window pops up with just a few sentences of plain text. You read and reread those sentences, then look at the ceiling and sigh. Looks like you're not going to bed tonight after all.

TURN TO

P. 165

S ❶ ACHIEVEMENT UNLOCKED
HERO

YOU WALK SLOWLY toward the flickering light and push past caution tape to reveal a staircase. You creep down the stairs, but can't make it all the way to the bottom thanks to several feet of standing water.

By squinting, you can make out old crates bobbing in the water. Looks like a storage room. Red light is coming from a hole in the wall on the opposite side of the room. Maybe that's where you need to go. You cringe and step into the water.

GLUCK. GLUCK. GLUCK.

Great, now you're going to have soggy socks. Halfway across the room, you feel something brush past your leg. Whoa! You jump on top of a crate and shine your light into the water. Too murky to see anything. Wait, something seems to be mov—

SNAP!

A giant red piranha flops onto your crate and tries to chomp your arm. "AHHH!" You kick it back into the water and start paddling toward the steps. Another piranha flops onto the crate. And then another. And another. You kick them off, but all your flailing tips you into the water.

E ❗ ACHIEVEMENT UNLOCKED
PIRANHA TANK
RETURN TO CHECKPOINT ON P. 76

HAWKE'S GRENADE LAUNCHER hasn't failed him yet. You pick it up, and a piece of the gnarled metal behind you starts glowing. Wait, does the game actually want you to shoot a grenade inside your own plane? And this is somehow supposed to make things better? The spot glows brighter. You take a deep breath and squeeze the trigger.

THUNK! BOOM!

The grenade gets lodged in the twisted metal and explodes. Congratulations, you've just blown a giant hole in your plane. Your survival instincts are top-notch. The hole starts sucking everything out, including the wingsuit.

"NOW WHAT?!" you scream.

You hear a creak, then the back half of the plane blows completely off.

"AHHHHHHHH!"

Thwipthwipthwipthwip!

You look down. A blue tarp underneath your seat is trying to escape. It must be important because it's glowing. You desperately start fishing it out, but then—*thwiiiiiiiip!*—the wind catches it, and it flies out of your hand. Before it can escape the plane, however, one of its metal grommets snags a hook. Now, it's trailing your plane like a streamer. Another hook behind the copilot's chair starts glowing, and suddenly, the video game's dumb plan clicks together. You're supposed to climb up there, snag the tarp, then hook it to the other side of the plane to create a giant parachute.

Seriously? Even for a video game, this is unrealistic. You wrap your legs around the pilot's seat, wrangle the tarp, and connect it to the other hook.

WHOOSH!

The tarp inflates into a parachute. You slow down, but not nearly enough. Your radio crackles. "Coop! What's going on?!"

You recognize the voice as Landra Lovato, Cooper's former treasure-hunting rival and current love interest. You grab the radio without considering how silly it is that seven-eighths of the airplane is gone, but the radio still works perfectly. "AHHHH-HHHH!"

"Redgrave's men must have shot you down! Do you still have those rafts?"

"WHAT ARE YOU TALKING ABOUT?!"

A compartment above the pilot's seat starts glowing. You open it, and uninflated life rafts start flying in your face. "HEY! HEY!"

You get knocked off your seat and find yourself briefly weightless. Then—*WOOMF!* You hit the tarp. You're now looking 20 feet down into the cockpit, surrounded by emergency life rafts. You pull a tab on the closest one. *FOOMP!* It inflates. You roll over to the next raft and pull the tab. *FOOMP!* Then the next raft. *FOOMP!* You glance down. The ground is coming up fast. You start moving in hyperspeed. *FOOMP! FOOMP! FOOMP!*

CRASH!

The crash is much more realistic than you'd like. The pile of rafts acts as a giant airbag, but you still hurt all over. "Helllllp," you moan.

"Hmmmhmmmhmmmhmmm."

Oh no. You've heard that evil chuckle before. You scramble out of the wreckage as fast as you can, but as soon as you emerge, something stings your neck. You pull out a small blow dart. Then you feel woozy. "Wharsh dish?" Your mouth doesn't work. "Barblarbdarb." The world starts going hazy, then snaps back for one second when a face pops into view.

"Nasty fall."

It's Declan Redgrave. You try to throw a punch but can't even move your arm. That's the last thing you remember before passing out.

TURN TO

P. 36

! ACHIEVEMENT UNLOCKED
TOP-NOTCH SURVIVAL INSTINCTS

YOU PRESS FORWARD, hopping and balancing and sweating more than you've ever sweat in your life. Finally, you reach the other side of the room and make a shocking discovery. That's not a tunnel you've been hopping toward. It's a waterfall. A waterfall made of lava. A lavafall.

You turn around, but you're too late. Your platform has broken free and is now speeding toward the lavafall. You duck and cover your head when you tip over the edge, but, miraculously, not a drop of lava splashes on you when you land. Even more miraculously, you spot something white and shining stuck to a stalactite. OK, seriously? A Shandling page way down here? You snatch the page when you drift underneath the stalactite.

Your heart rate picks up when you finish the note. What's going on? No time to figure it out now—the lava has begun flowing faster. You run from side to side to steer the platform around stalactites falling from the ceiling, fireballs shooting from the lava, and killer bats hiding on the walls.

Right when you think you can't take any more, the platform crashes through a wall and throws you overboard. You tumble onto the ground and raise your fist in triumph. There it is on a pedestal: a glowing red stone shaped like an apple.

"ROAR!"

An orange monster drops in front of you. Oh, come on!

"ROOOOAAAAAAAR!"

You look up to see four more monsters hanging on a stalactite above you. Great. It's a boss battle, and you don't have anything to protect yourself. You step backward and trip over something. It's your trusty grenade launcher! It must have fallen down here through a different tunnel.

May 30, 1975

My men are gone. All of them. Overnight. Disappeared.

I left them yesterday morning in good spirits. This morning, in their place, are . . . I do not dare describe the horrible creatures. I am fortunate to have escaped with my life.

My mind is tortured with the possibilities. Did something crack deep within the earth to let the monsters escape? Did the creatures wait until my team slept to rise from the great pit? Were my men tortured?

There appears to be no sign of struggle, which leads me to one last possibility, more terrifying than any of the others. Perhaps my men are not gone after all. Perhaps they are the monsters.

—William K. Shandling

You pick up the weapon and aim at the monster's chest. Just before you pull the trigger, you pause. These monsters look like they're big fans of edenberries. If that's true, their reflexes are going to be way too fast for your grenade launcher. You need a sneakier plan. You aim your launcher a little bit right, then fire. The monster can't help itself. It dives toward the grenade, picks it out of the air, and throws it back at you. You're ready for the return, though. Since the monster had to dive to catch the grenade, you have enough time to roll out of the way.

BOOM!

The explosion blows a hole in the ground and seems to disorient the monster. The giant creature roars again and stumbles toward you, rubbing its eyes. It doesn't see the hole and tumbles down it. Two more monsters jump down to avenge their fallen friend. Well, it worked the first time. You fire two more grenades, let the monsters throw them back at you, then watch them stumble through the holes they create. You repeat the process until all the monsters are gone.

When you finish, the cavern floor is mostly holes. It seems barely strong enough to hold you. Then, the ground starts to rumble. You sprint toward the stone and dive on it before everything falls apart. The stone flashes the number three, then everything goes white, and you're transported back to the island.

TURN TO
P. 54

❶ ACHIEVEMENT UNLOCKED
MONSTER MASH

THAT'S THE WRONG CHOICE. You die. This makes you so sad that you write a haiku about it. (A haiku is a three-line poem with exactly 17 syllables—five in the first line, seven in the second, and five in the third.) Record your poem in the space provided below.

_____

Five syllables

_____

Seven syllables

_____

Five syllables

Your haiku is so touching that it moves everyone who reads it to tears. Turn it in as your next school project, regardless of the class, for an instant A.

E › **● ACHIEVEMENT UNLOCKED**
POET LAUREATE
RETURN TO CHECKPOINT ON P. 113

"WAKE UP, SLEEPY." *Ooooof.* Everything's still foggy. "Sleeeeeeepy, wake uuuuuuup." Something brushes your face. You try to slap it away, but your hands are tied behind your back. You finally open your eyes to find that you're trapped in a harshly lit metal box with Declan Redgrave. You want to say something witty, but you can't with all the bouncing and rocking. Must be a truck. The motion sickness makes you close your eyes again.

"Few people on Earth could survive that fall, but I knew you would. I was counting on it, actually. You see, I need to talk to you. Not Landra, not your precious grenade launcher, but you, Cooper Hawke. We're not so different, you and I . . ."

You're glad that your eyes are closed so Declan can't see you roll your eyes. A message appears in the darkness: Fast-forward through this scene by saying "skip." ·

SELECT

61 Skip the annoying monologue.

65 Listen.

YOU JUMP OFF the waterfall and plunge into the water below. It's so cold! The programmers could have made it any temperature they wanted, and they chose ice?! You wipe your eyes and try to catch your breath from the shock, only to get another shock: enormous red fish with crooked teeth are speeding toward you. These steroid piranhas are chomping everything in their path, including each other.

Rock walls on both sides of the river are fencing you in. Your only option is to duck underneath the waterfall and hope these fish have a weird thing about water falling on their heads.

Fortunately, you're in a video game, and in video games, there's always something behind waterfalls. In this case, it's a small cave. The piranhas follow you in, but you scramble to dry land before they can reach you. You're safe for now, but you've got to figure out a way out of here that doesn't involve getting back in that water.

In the corner of the cave is an orange, spiky berry that matches Shandling's description of an edenberry. Above your head are vines hanging from the ceiling. Which do you choose?

SELECT

87 Eat the edenberry.

14 Try to Tarzan on the vines.

YOU FIND THE KEY, dive down, and unlock the door. The flood spits you into one final room with a pedestal holding a glowing berry idol. You dive for the idol, but just before you reach it, the pedestal flips over, replacing the idol with a stone that's covered in symbols.

It takes you a minute to decipher the puzzle, but you eventually recognize it as sudoku. In a sudoku puzzle, each row, column, and large square can only have one of each symbol. You must use the symbols provided to deduce where the rest go.

With this particular puzzle, you're not done when you finish the sudoku. Use the math clues to figure out the number that each shape represents. Put together the three numerals from the highlighted boxes to arrive at a three-digit number. This is the page number you must turn to.

That's a lot of work, huh? And you're running out of time too. The room is almost filled with water. Just as things start feeling hopeless, you spot an edenberry in the corner of the room. Do you take the brain boost and skip this puzzle?

SELECT

93 Eat edenberry.

39 Complete puzzle.

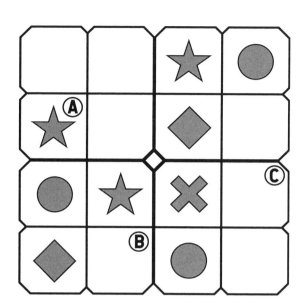

★ = 1   ★ + ◆ = 10

◆ =   ◆ − ● = 6

✖ =   ● + ● + ✖ + ✖ + ★ = 7

● =

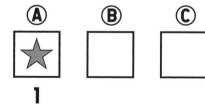

TURN TO P. __1__ ____ ____

As you may have discovered, this game's artificial intelligence is unbeatable. You may feel like you're trapped forever. You're not. I've found a glitch in the game.

Find the mirror in the wall that's "stuck." The image it shows will be slightly behind all the others. Press this mirror and hum the highest note you can. If your hum matches the frequency of the book's hum, you'll break the game.

Good luck.

TURN TO

P.25

YOU GO FOR the club because it's an actual weapon you can use to defend yourself. When you bend over to pick it up, you get a nice view of the jungle below you through a hole in the floor. Then, quicker than you can blink, you get a nice view of something else.

CHOMP!

The snake shoots through the hole and swallows you before you can lift the club off your shoulders.

A ❗ ACHIEVEMENT UNLOCKED
NICE VIEW
RETURN TO CHECKPOINT ON P. 56

YOU FIND SHALLOW grooves in the tree and start climbing to the nest as fast as you can. The bird swoops down several times to make things difficult for you, but you manage to avoid its attacks and climb all the way to the branch. By the time you make it, your arms are shaking, and your fingers are cramping. You run to the nest. Maybe there are eggs in here you can throw like Yoshi.

You lean over the nest and quickly recoil. The eggs have already cracked open to reveal orange-eyed baby monster birds. They start chirping excitedly when they see you. Then, when you raise your grenade launcher, the chirping stops. They realize you're not their mom coming back with a meal, and they're not happy about it.

Before you can pull the trigger, the launcher gets snatched out of your hands. Big mama has it. Then, she flips you into the nest. Dinner is served after all.

❶ ACHIEVEMENT UNLOCKED
YOU'RE NOT YOSHI
RETURN TO CHECKPOINT ON P. 90

THE LIGHTNING PROVIDED just enough light for you to spot another tentacle 20 feet below you. This one also looks like a roller-coaster track, but it doesn't lead to the vortex, so it's probably a better choice. As soon as you notice the tentacle, you feel the hand disappear. Creepy. Maybe it was an angel. Are there video game angels?

No time to think about it now. You shift your weight and roll onto the second tentacle. This one is much narrower, so you grip the board tighter and try to keep your balance. You wobble a bit as the tentacle gets skinnier. It's so dark that you can't see anything now, so you trust that you're on the right path. Suddenly, you swoop into the air. The tentacle's taking you for a loop the loop. You hang on all the way through the loop and then go weightless.

You suck in air and hold your breath as you prepare to crash-land into the ocean. As you tumble through the air, you lose track of which way is up. Finally, you land on your back. Hard. You brace yourself to get swallowed by the cold sea, but the water never comes. Instead, you smack your head on sand and get knocked unconscious.

When you finally reopen your eyes, it's morning. You're lying on a beach surrounded by the sound of birds chirping and waves gently washing on shore. Phantom Island. You made it.

You rub your head, sit up, and gasp. The ocean in front of you is filled with long, thick vines. Some are winding around each other, some are floating lazily in the waves, and others almost look like they're waving to you. Wait. Maybe those weren't kraken tentacles last night. Could they have been giant vines? If so, where did they come from?

You turn around and get your answer. Phantom Island features stunning waterfalls, dramatic cliffs, and exotic flowers. But the only thing you notice when you get your first glimpse of the island—the only thing anyone could possibly notice—is the tree.

You're no arborist, but you immediately know that the tree at the center of Phantom Island would have to set the record for biggest tree on Earth. It's thicker than a house. Maybe thicker than a mansion. The trunk stretches to dizzying heights before its branches spread out into a canopy so large that it shades the entire island. Whatever the secret of Phantom Island is, it's got to have something to do with that tree.

You stand up and stretch. You're sore, sandy, and still a little soggy, but for pretty much the first time since you got into this dumb game, you're not in immediate danger, so you feel great. You take a deep breath while you strap your grenade launcher to your back and shake your head in admiration when you smell beach. Bionosoft really went all out for this one.

You take a few steps down the beach and notice a glowing piece of paper sticking out of the sand. You've learned by now that glowing things are important, so you pick it up. Looks like it's an entry from someone's diary. You read it, then stuff it into your pocket and continue on your way.

> *Journal entries like the one you see on the right contain clues that will help you understand Phantom Island. Be sure to read each one you find.*

You're so wrapped up in the beauty of the island that you don't notice a root in your path.

Crack.

May 16, 1975

After decades spent chasing dead ends and fables, I have arrived. The legends are real. Phantom Island exists.

The island is more beautiful than I ever imagined. It is a modern-day Garden of Eden. My team will need years to study all the new species of flora and fauna on the island. In fact, we may need years to study the very first item we found.

Almost immediately after we landed, one of my men brought me a peculiar berry. It was orange in color, covered in small spikes, and appeared to glow. "Reckon it's safe to eat?" he asked. At that moment, an inquisitive squirrel with a blue stripe down its back met us. I gave the berry to the squirrel, and something extraordinary happened. Upon eating the fruit, the squirrel's eyes began glowing orange. Then, it walked on its front paws. It leaped into the air and completed a series of stunning acrobatic maneuvers. It even juggled three nearby pebbles. After two minutes had passed, the squirrel's eyes returned to normal, and it scampered away.

I have decided to name the berry "edenberry." I also believe that I shall keep the squirrel as my personal pet and name him "Ringo."

—William K. Shandling

The breeze stops blowing. Birds stop chirping. It feels like the entire island is holding its breath. You look down and see that all you did was snap a thin root. Suddenly, you get goose bumps. You spin around. The vines in the ocean aren't drooping anymore. They're all standing straight up. Well, that was a pleasant, danger-free 30 seconds.

You take a step backward. One of the vines points at you and moves forward. You take another step, and a second vine joins its friend. That's it. You turn and run.

Fffwthhh!

You've never heard the sound of vines chasing someone before, but you'd bet all the money in the world that's what "fffwthhh" is. You steal a glance behind you and immediately wish you hadn't. The vines have twisted together to form a super-vine with a pointy drill tip. Also, they're moving surprisingly fast.

The beach turns to jungle, which turns into a steep uphill climb. You run as fast as you can, but the heavy grenade launcher on your back is really slowing you down. You finally make it over a hill, which gives you a few seconds of cover from the super-vine. You look for options while trying to catch your breath. To your left is a small waterfall. If you jump off it, you might be able to lose the vines. To your right is a cave. Maybe you can hide in there. Where do you go?

SELECT

37 Waterfall.

84 Cave.

THE GIANT MACHINE pushes the anvil off the ledge, which launches the boulder into the basket and opens the door. You step through the door and immediately fall down a hole into something that looks like an ancient cannon.

Whirr. The cannon slowly lowers until it is pointing at an empty hallway. You try wriggling out, but you're stuck. *Whirr.* The cannon turns right. Now it's pointing at a hallway with a thousand buzzing saws. *Whirr.* Another right turn. This hallway is filled with pointy spears. *Whirr.* Another right turn. This isn't a hallway—it's a bottomless pit. *Whirr.* One final right turn points you back at the empty hallway.

The doors all close, and the cannon turns left two clicks, right three clicks, left, right, left, left, right five clicks, left four clicks, then pauses before clicking left one last time. Finally, a control panel appears in front of you. How do you get to the clear hallway? You have 10 seconds to decide.

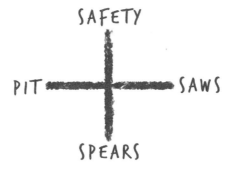

SELECT

88	Fire now.
72	Right.
35	Left.
96	Flip.

YOU AIM AT the gorilla's giant chest, squeeze the trigger, and raise your arms in victory before the grenade even hits its target. How could you miss?! That chest is massive.

Here's exactly how you can miss: your opponent has been snorking down edenberries, and he's really fast. The gorilla uses his lightning-quick edenberry reflexes to snatch the grenade out of the air before it reaches him, then he throws it back at you. You, unfortunately, do not have lightning-quick reflexes, and therefore explode.

0 ❗ ACHIEVEMENT UNLOCKED
EARLY CELEBRATION
RETURN TO CHECKPOINT ON P. 16

YOU SHOVE A plum-size edenberry into your mouth.

WHOOSH!

The effects feel even stronger this time. Suddenly, you know who killed John F. Kennedy. You know all the ingredients of Coke. Most importantly, you know the map to this insane underground maze. You sprint past the monster, tear through the kitchen, and skid to a stop in the main lab. You notice two things you missed the first time you were here: a rope to your left and a giant stalactite above you. You tie a lariat loop (even though you couldn't explain what that is or how to tie it), lasso the stalactite with perfect aim, then start climbing.

The monster jumps onto a desk and dives at you, but you swing at the last second, and the monster takes down the stalactite instead. The rock breaks through the floor to reveal a volcanic vent underneath. You jump into the vent, navigate a maze of tunnels, then roll into a cavern right in front of a glowing red stone shaped like an apple. The stone flashes the number three when you pick it up. Then, everything fades and you return to the clearing.

TURN TO

P.54

❶ ACHIEVEMENT UNLOCKED
MAP MASTER

THE EFFECTS OF the berry wear off just as you step into a clearing. You lean on a tree to steady yourself. Did that really happen? It feels like you've got a heartbeat in your head and just rode a rickety roller coaster. You wait a few moments for the feeling to pass, then look up. This is *THE* tree, isn't it?

Up close, the tree is impossibly huge. The trunk is so thick and tall that looking up feels like you're staring at a wall that stretches to heaven. You take a few steps back to get a better look, and something squishes under your foot. It's an edenberry. In fact, there are bright, orange edenberries everywhere you look.

You pick up one of the berries to get a closer look. The first thing you notice is it's not tingling in your hand anymore. This time, a warm, comforting feeling seems to spread from the fruit. You lift the berry to your face and squint. Does it really have its own light? You cup your other hand over the berry and peek inside. Yup, it's definitely glowing on its own. And in the dark, the small spikes cast weird shadows.

"Eat it." You hear your own voice in your head as clearly as if you spoke the words yourself. You look around for someone else, but you're still alone. You look back at the berry. Might as well, right? What's the harm in trying another power-up?

You pop the berry into your mouth.

WHOOSH!

Time slows, and suddenly, you know the secret of Phantom Island. You see the cube mirror room again, and you realize it's inside the tree. You must get there. You jump on the tree and start climbing using only your fingers. Once you're 20 feet off the ground, you try to tear into the bark with your fingernails. When you realize that's not working, you hop down and start running.

You're bounding like a deer now. You know 54 strides will get you there. Where's "there"? Your conscious brain hasn't caught up yet, but you're sure it's going to be great.

On your 54th stride, you reach the other side of the tree and smile. You've found a door carved into the tree. A few feet from the tree is a circular stone platform divided into three colors: red, green, and blue. As soon as you see the stone, you know that each color represents a different challenge. You also know that you must complete all three challenges to open the tree's door. This is definitely the only way out of the game.

Wow, those are all helpful facts to magically pop into your head! Unfortunately, they're accompanied by about a million extremely unhelpful facts. For example, you now know that 97 is the square root of 9,409. You know that Colorado Rockies outfielder Dante Bichette had a .304 batting average in 1994. You know that Munfordville is a Kentucky municipality with a population of 1,653 and a Sonic that serves especially good frozen cherry limeades. (That last fact might actually turn out to be helpful if you ever find yourself on a road trip down Interstate 65 with a hankering for a tasty treat.)

The stream of information entering your brain becomes so intense that you hold your head to keep it from overwhelming you. Flies hum in the key of F! Juicy Fruit gum was the first product to use a bar code! Astronaut Buzz Aldrin's mother's maiden name was "Moon!" Another Shandling page is right behind you!

The last fact echoes in your brain as the berry's effects subside. You turn, and sure enough, there's another glowing piece of paper 20 yards away. You shake your head as you pick it up. Only in a video game do people leave individual pages of their personal diaries lying around, and only in a video game could those pages remain readable 45 years later.

You frown when you finish the note. Shandling doesn't sound like he's OK. You wince. That heartbeat in your head is more like a headache now, and your chest is buzzing. Then, you notice your fingernails and start to get worried. They're bloody from trying to tear into the tree earlier. What came over you? You decide it's probably best to lay off the berries until you learn more about them.

You turn your attention to the stone on the ground.

TURN TO

P. 54

May 21, 1975

My team has accomplished a task that I imagined would require a lifetime. We have built an underground research laboratory and documented every species of flora and fauna on Phantom Island. How could that be possible in only five days? The edenberry.

I have no doubt that the edenberry will change the course of human history. It can turn even the most milquetoast into Superman in a moment. Every time I experience the power of the berry, I regret the years I wasted without it. Everyone here has taken to the berries, but especially Ringo. The squirrel has eaten so many berries that his blue stripe has turned orange. He now becomes violent when he cannot have a berry, and I for one do not blame him!

The berries have revealed to me that my singular focus must be entering the island's tree. The tree contains the secret of the universe. It has been three days since I have slept, for I cannot rest until I know what is inside the tree.

I must now draw this entry to a close. My hand has become unsteady. Perhaps another edenberry will help.

—William K. Shandling

THE STONE IS divided into three colors that represent three different challenges. You can complete the challenges in any order. Which do you choose?

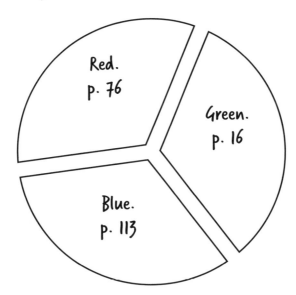

When you complete each challenge, you'll be rewarded with a number. Fill in all three numbers below to learn which page to turn to next.

TURN TO P. _____ _____ _____

YOU SQUEEZE THE TRIGGER, but not before the monster gets in a punch. The hit throws you off balance, which causes your grenade to shoot harmlessly to the side. At least, the grenade seems harmless until it explodes. The explosion destroys a chunk of the platform you both are on. The monster stares at the ceiling and groans, "I was on your side."

Wait, what?! The platform rumbles and falls, sending you both down the pit.

E ❗ ACHIEVEMENT UNLOCKED
FRIENDLY MONSTER
RETURN TO CHECKPOINT ON P. 136

YOU GRAB THE snake's tail. It's skinny and squirmy and super gross. You ignore all that and yank it toward the snake's gaping mouth. By now, the creature is out of control with its thrashing and snapping. You tug the tail as hard as you can, but it gets stuck a few feet short. You squat and pull harder. When you turn your back to the snake, it lunges.

CHOMP!

The snake gets a mouthful of its own tail.

"EEEEEEE!"

It shrieks. Wait, is that a real snake thing? You make a mental note to find out if snakes actually shriek when you get out of this game. The snake temporarily loosens its grip on the house, causing its body to sag, which reveals the door. You climb over the snake, sprint through the door, and start running across the rope bridge to the next tree house.

As you run, you peek behind you in time to see the snake unravel itself from the tree house and disappear into the leaf canopy. That can't be good. You hear rustling leaves directly overhead, then—*WHOMP!*—a giant snake head drops in front of you, fang-first. You stop just in time to dodge the mouth, then continue when the snake goes back into the tree. You dodge three more attacks before arriving at the next tree house.

You slam the door, then groan. This house has cracks and holes everywhere. You duck so the snake can't see you through the window and creep toward the back door.

CRACK!

The snake's head breaks through the wall in front of you. You stumble backward and kick it in the chin. The snake shakes its head and disappears again. Before you can start moving—*CRACK*—it bursts through the opposite wall. You roll into the next room and slam the door. This room has two items in it: a club and an old, broken mirror. Which do you pick up?

SELECT

41 Club.

59 Mirror.

GREEN MEANS GO. Go is good. That is your entire reason for choosing the green tunnel. You stick your head into the skinny tunnel, and the rest of your body gets sucked in. The tunnel zips you all around until you get dizzy. It's like one of those bank money tubes, except if the bank decided to make a real fun ride for the money. Finally, it spits you into a cavern.

Every square inch of the cavern is covered in glowing green and blue mushrooms. The patch of green mushrooms you're standing on is squishy, so you bounce on them. One little bounce sends you 30 feet up to the ceiling. Up here, gravity is reversed, so you stick to the ceiling. You jump again, and gravity switches again.

On the fourth jump, you land on a blue mushroom instead of green. You try another jump, but you're stuck. The blue mushrooms are made of some sort of alien goo that's crawling up your leg! You tear your leg away, but now the goo is crawling after you. Where do you go?! There's a tunnel to your left that's glowing red and a tunnel to your right that's bright like daylight.

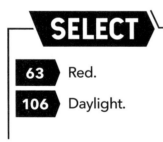

SELECT

63 Red.

106 Daylight.

YOU GRAB THE mirror and wait for the snake to poke its dumb head through another crack, but it never does. You glance at the mirror while you wait. The face looking back at you is your own. Not Cooper Hawke, but you-you. You touch the mirror, and the face winks, even though you're almost positive you didn't wink. Then, the mirror gets blocky like it has a glitch and reassembles itself. But your face isn't in the mirror anymore. It's Cooper Hawke.

CREEEEEEEAAAAAK.

Unfortunately, you don't have time to investigate that superweird thing that just happened because the snake is doing its house-squeezing thing again.

CRACK!

The flimsy tree house breaks in two, and suddenly the snake has you wrapped up. It looks you in the eye and starts swaying. Your arms feel heavy, but you know this is your only chance. You hold up the mirror and close your eyes. Nothing happens. You finally peek and see the snake staring at itself in the mirror with its eyes all googly and mouth hanging slack. It's hypnotized itself! You squirm out of the snake's hold, carefully set down the mirror, and creep out of the house. Once you reach the rope bridge, you wipe the sweat off your forehead and start jogging.

Bzzzzzzzz.

You pick up the pace when you hear a buzzing electricity sound behind you. What's coming this time? A robot monkey? A giant dragonfly, perhaps? You finally look back. It's a black cloud.

Now, black clouds are not usually too scary unless you're planning a picnic, but you quickly figure out that this cloud isn't bringing rain. It's a swarm of killer bees! You start running as fast as you can. Halfway across the bridge, you realize that the buzzing is getting quieter. You're actually outrunning the bees. Aren't bees supposed to be fast? You turn to see that the swarm isn't chasing you anymore. Instead, it has settled on the bridge's ropes.

CRACK!

The left rope snaps. Oh. Oh no. Before you can grab hold of something, the bees finish their job, and the bridge falls. You try to hold on and swing like you did before, but you can't get a grip and tumble into the abyss. You look down to see that you actually have two options for breaking your fall. There's the roof of a lower-level tree house to your right and a nest of purple Venus flytrap-looking plants to your left. Where do you go?

SELECT

138 Monster plants.

108 Roof.

DECLAN STARTS SPEEDING through his villain monologue.

"Wewantthesamethingsoutoflife. Ithinkthat'sobvious. Butwhat'salsopainfullyobviousisthatyoudon'thavethegutstogetthem. That'sOKHawke.I'mheretohelpyou. Lookatme. Whereisthemap? Listentoyourself. 'Whatmap?' Don'tplaydumbwithmeHawke. Thisisyourlastwarning. Webothknowwhatmap I'mtalkingabout. That'sright. ThemaptoPhantomIsland. Mywholelife I'veheardrumorsaboutanislandwithasecretsobigthatit'sbeenerasedfromeveryglobeintheworld. Asecretthat'sdrivencenturiesofexplorerstomadness. AndnowthatI'vefoundthe-ShandlingdiaryIknowtherumorsaretrue. Youknowwhat I'mtalkingaboutbecauseyou'vereadthediarytoohaven'tyouHawke? Don'tactsosurprised. IfollowedShandling'scluestotheonlyplaceintheworldthemapcouldbeandit'sgone. Thatcanonlymeanonethingyouhaveit. SotellmewhereisitHawke? Youdidn'tdestroyit. Iknowyoudidn't. Youknowwhy? Becauseiknowyou. AndyoumayhavegottenscaredyoumayhavedecidedinyourinfinitewisdomthatnooneshouldevergotoPhantomIslandbutIcanguaranteethatyoudidn'tdestroyit. Youhidit. There'sasmallpartofyouthatneedstoknowwhat'sonthatislandyourself. Sodoyouhavesomethingtotellme? Nowdoyouhavesomethingtotellme? GRENADE!"

BOOM!

An explosion rocks the truck, and you die.

Wait! That's a cheap death. How could you have known that was going to happen?! Go back and read the last word of the part you just skipped to find out. Now, stop being in such a hurry and enjoy the book.

T ❗ ACHIEVEMENT UNLOCKED
PATIENCE IS A VIRTUE
RETURN TO CHECKPOINT ON P. 36

YOU GRAB THE EDENBERRY just as the wolf springs into action. The fruit makes your hand tingle, but you stuff it into your mouth anyway. Whoa. Your eyes bug open, almost like they're going to pop out of your head. Time slows way down, and your brain feels like it's received a shot of adrenaline. This is an amazing power-up! You look at the wolf and suddenly realize that if you perform an Eagle strike followed by a Kimura hold, you can decommission the animal. Also, you somehow know what "Eagle strike," "Kimura hold," and "decommission" mean. You pull off your martial arts moves like a black belt, then kick the wolf into the vine.

Next, you take off through the cave system. Even though you're horrible at directions, you know these tunnels like you were raised in them. Also, you have night vision, because why not. Along the way, you ballerina your way through a gauntlet of shooting flames, somersault over a nest of glowing spiders, and decommission 18 more wolves. Finally, there's light at the end of the tunnel. You don't know where you're headed, but your berry brain seems to have a destination in mind.

TURN TO

P. 50

A ❗ ACHIEVEMENT UNLOCKED
INSTANT BLACK BELT

YOU CHOOSE THE red tunnel because this is the red challenge, and you're really hoping the glow is coming from your prize and not fire. Once you crawl through the tube, you find . . . fire. Lots and lots of fire.

A lake of magma stretches in front of you. This must be the heart of the volcano. Platforms are bobbing on the lava, inviting you to hop across. You usually wouldn't trust something floating just inches above boiling lava, but you know that no adventure game is complete without a lava platforming section.

Once you start hopping across the lava, you recognize a problem. These gaps are made for a Cooper Hawke-size person with Cooper Hawke athletic ability. You have neither. Each leap leads to a mini heart attack. Do you really want to try hopping all the way across? Looks like there are two tunnels nearby—one that's shining bright like daylight, and another skinny one that's glowing green. What do you want to do?

SELECT

32 Keep going.

58 Green tunnel.

106 Bright tunnel.

YOU KNOW WHAT? Maybe the bees aren't so bad after all. Beekeepers are friends with them, right? Maybe it's time to make some new pals. You pry open the plant and poke out your head. A massive swarm of killer bees starts swirling like a tornado.

"Hey guys," you try. "I know we got off on the wrong foot earlier, but I wanted to let you know I love bees. I'm even friends with one. You might know him. His name is . . . well, I'm not sure exactly what his name is, but he's the mascot for Honey Nut Cheerios, which is probably the best version of Cheerios. Anyway, he wears tennis shoes and . . ."

That's as far as you get. You see, most bees hate BuzzBee, the Honey Nut Cheerios mascot. They think he's gone Hollywood. The bees express their hatred for BuzzBee by stinging you a thousand times. It hurts a great deal.

❶ ACHIEVEMENT UNLOCKED
HOLLYWOOD BUZZBEE
RETURN TO CHECKPOINT ON P. 138

"WE WANT THE same things out of life. I think that's obvious. But what's also painfully obvious is that you don't have the guts to get them. That's OK, Hawke. I'm here to help you. Look at me." You open your eyes. Declan's pointy face is close now. Too close. He's got a creepy thin-lipped smile. "Where is the map?"

"OK, so actually, hi, I'm not Cooper Hawke," you say. "I got into this video game through a weird book, which I thought would be fun, but it turns out to be super not fun, soooooo, what do you know about getting out of here?"

Declan smirks. "Listen to yourself. 'What map?' Don't play dumb with me, Hawke."

"I didn't . . . Wait, you can't hear me, can you?"

Declan smacks your face. "This is your last warning. We both know what map I'm talking about."

This is disappointing. You expected more from Declan with all the talk about advanced artificial intelligence, but he can't understand you at all. Declan's basically a robot programmed to recite scripted lines no matter what you say, which means you could say anything right now. How about, "Your face looks like a chewed-up pencil, and your breath smells like dog burps."

Declan smiles. "That's right. The map to Phantom Island. My whole life, I've heard rumors about an island with a secret so big that it's been erased from every globe in the world. A secret that's driven centuries of explorers to madness. And now that I've found the Shandling diary, I know the rumors are true. You know what I'm talking about because you've read the diary too, haven't you, Hawke?"

"No, but I've read your diary, so I know that you
_____."

Make up something embarrassing that Declan might write in his diary.

Declan does not look shocked. Instead, he looks downright smug. "Don't act so surprised. I followed Shandling's clues to the only place in the world the map could be, and it's gone. That means one thing: you have it. So, tell me. Where is it, Hawke?"

"_____."

Insert ridiculous or slightly rude location.

Declan shakes his head. "You didn't destroy it. I know you didn't. You know why? Because I know you. And you may have gotten scared, you may have decided in your infinite wisdom that no one should ever go to Phantom Island, but I can guarantee that you didn't destroy it. You hid it. There's a small part of you that needs to know what's on that island. So, do you have something to tell me?"

"_____."

Insert joke about Declan's mom.

Declan arches his eyebrow and pulls out a knife. "*Now* do you have something to tell me?"

You gulp. The sight of a knife, even a video game one, drains all your confidence. "Look, I just . . ."

THUNK.

Declan looks at the ceiling in horror. "GRENADE!"

SELECT

68 Dive out of the way.

EVEN THOUGH YOU'RE tied to a chair, you do your best to roll out of the way. You end up tipping over.

> *Turn the book upside down to continue.*
> *When you finish the page, flip it back over.*

BOOM!

The roof explodes, and the truck screeches to a halt. There's smoke everywhere. Moonlight streams through a hole in the roof. Suddenly, Landra's face appears in the hole.

"Drop the knife, Declan!" she yells.

Declan sighs, lays down the knife, and stands up. "You could have just knocked."

Landra lowers herself through the hole but doesn't see what you see from your perspective on the floor. Declan is hiding a second knife in his other hand!

"NO!" You try to sweep Declan's legs before he can attack Landra.

The move doesn't knock Declan over or anything, but it does distract him long enough for Landra to grab his hand and twist it around his neck. "Drop it."

Declan drops his second knife, and Landra kicks it to you. "Let's go."

Landra waits patiently while you fumble with the knife. Once you finally free yourself, she boosts you through the hole. "Pleasure as always, Declan," she says as she hoists herself onto the roof and rolls off the truck in one smooth motion. You try copying her but end up falling face-first onto a grenade launcher she'd left on the road. You grab the weapon, rub your head, and follow Landra onto a nearby motorcycle.

VROOOOOOM!

Landra's quick start almost knocks you off the bike. As you pull yourself back up, you notice Declan throw the driver out of the truck and gun the engine. You quickly learn that this level is a chase where you're responsible for launching well-placed grenades to slow Declan, clear debris, and open new routes. After a shaky start, you surprise yourself by holding your own while Landra drives like a maniac. Just as you start finding your groove, you cross a bridge and see a "road closed" barrier blocking a giant chasm in front of you. You've got a choice: blow up the bridge to get rid of Declan for good or knock down the barrier so Landra can use it as a ramp to jump the chasm. Decide now—you're moving fast.

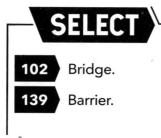

SELECT

| 102 | Bridge. |
| 139 | Barrier. |

YOU RUN ONTO the banana branch and lose your balance. It's so skinny! As you fall, you grab the branch and hang. The gorillas try swiping at you, but you're able to scoot to the banana cluster just out of reach. You're safe for now, but the branch is really sagging.

The biggest gorilla decides to give the branch a hearty shake-shake-shake. On the third shake, the bananas fly off, sending you soaring over the gorillas' heads. You tumble through the leaf canopy, then fly through the window of another tree house and land with a *SPLAT.*

Better get out of here before the apes catch up. You jog through the kitchen, reach for the front door, then pull back your hand when you hear something move on the other side.

Creeeeeeeeeeaaaaaaak.

The house starts creaking, but not normal creaking you hear when someone's walking upstairs. It almost sounds like something's about to snap.

CRASH!

You spin around. A shelf just fell, and the wall where it'd been seems to be bowing. Next, a crack starts forming. The crack spiders all the way up the wall, then—*BOOM!*—a giant snake head breaks through the wall. The snake spots you and starts swaying. You want to run, but you can't look away for some reason. You slowly backpedal until your foot hits a stair. That snaps you out of it, and you run up the winding staircase.

When you reach the top of the stairs, you look out a window and gasp. The snake has the whole tree house wrapped in its body like it's squeezing a can of soda. You climb out the window, then use the snake's body as a slide to get back down to the first story.

Back inside the house, you look for the door. That's when you feel a tickle in your ear.

"AHHHH!" You turn and see that it's the snake's tail. You slap it away, then almost run into the snake's mouth. It snaps, but the snake is so tangled in the house that it can't reach you. Now's your chance to take it out. What's your target?

SELECT

56 Tail.

82 Head.

YOU SHOOT DOWN a torch-lit hallway, then skid to a stop in front of a stone wall with a picture carved into it.

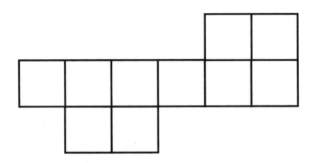

You edge forward to get a better look, but a trapdoor opens underneath you. You tumble into another room filled with thousands of golden, blocky shapes. Is this a treasure room? The only other thing in here is an oversized door with a glowing keyhole.

SHING! CLANG-CLANG-CLANG-CLANG.

The ceiling sprouts spikes and starts lowering toward you. You panic and look around. This isn't a treasure room. It's a key collection! You've got to find the one that matches the carving before it's too late. You collect six keys that look like they might match. Which one is correct?

Find the 3D key on the next page that matches the 2D side view above. Once you find the correct key, turn to the page number associated with it.

P.35

P.89

P.80

P.119

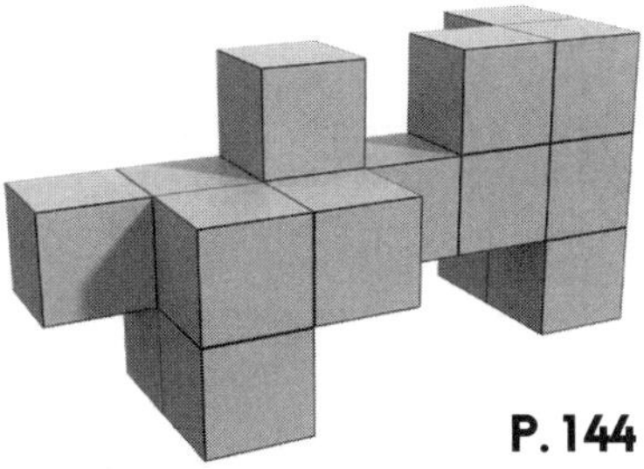

P.144

YOU GRAB THE vine and shimmy until you reach a greenhouse. What's the purpose of an underground greenhouse, anyway? There's no sun down here. That's a super question that you'd probably investigate were you not busy trying to keep down your lunch. This greenhouse stinks—and not just an everyday stink. It stinks like all the stinks in the world got together for a big party, then refused to take out the trash.

The smell is probably coming from all the dead plants. This room is home to at least 100 bizarre plants—plants with fangs, plants with tongues, plants that appear to have eyes—and they're all rotting. The only things living in this room are vines that have managed to break through the ceiling and walls.

You start feeling woozy and lean against a wall to steady yourself. The glass shatters from your weight, and warm air blows in. Thankful for the fresh air, you stick your head through the hole and consider your options. You could escape through this hole or climb a vine out of the room. Looks like there are three different vines—green, blue, and yellow.

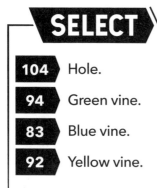

SELECT

104 Hole.

94 Green vine.

83 Blue vine.

92 Yellow vine.

YOUR CLONE SCOWLS. "You're either lying or bad at following directions. Either way, I don't have any use for you."

With that, the video game collapses in on you.

ACHIEVEMENT UNLOCKED

DO THE MATH

RETURN TO CHECKPOINT ON P. 153

YOU STEP ONTO the red section of the circle and wait for something to haaaaaaaaaaa—

The stone opens and plunges you into a hole. You tumble down a tunnel that twists and turns in pitch-black darkness. About halfway down, your grenade launcher snags on a rock, and the weapon tears off your body. Finally, the tunnel levels out, and you roll into a dark cavern.

You rub your head and put your shirt over your nose. It smells like you landed in an old person's cellar. You switch on your flashlight and blink. Did you go back in time? There's old-timey lab equipment and wooden crates everywhere.

"Gggggrrrrrrr."

What was that? You shut off your flashlight and duck behind a crate. After a few moments of silence, you shine your light back at the tunnel, and your heart sinks. Your grenade launcher didn't make it. But you do spot something. Looks like a map. You pick it up. Gulp. Someone added a bunch of scary stuff and a dire warning to this particular map.

A light flickers to your right. You hear growling ahead, this time a little closer. You stuff the map in your pocket. Time to move. Where do you go?

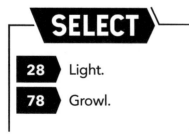

SELECT

28 Light.

78 Growl.

YOU FIGHT YOUR body's instincts and slowly walk toward the growling. The next room appears to be the main hub of the research station. Rows of workbenches and tall 1970s computer towers are arranged in a maze.

"GRRRRRRRR."

Something moves to your left, and you duck underneath a desk just in time. The green glow from a nearby computer illuminates a gruesome monster. It's six feet tall with an oversized head and long fingers that end in claws, but the thing that really captures your attention is its fur. The creature is covered from head to toe in stringy, tangled orange fur.

You hold your breath, and the monster passes by. Now's your chance. You scramble to the middle of the room, then glance at your map. Looks like you can continue on to the living quarters, the kitchen, or a hallway of offices. You turn around to get your bearings and bump into a rolling office chair.

SQUEAK!

The sound echoes through the lab, and the monster stops walking. Move! Now!

SELECT

83 Living quarters.

85 Kitchen.

86 Offices.

YOU CHOOSE THE correct key and open the lock just in time. As soon as you enter the next room, the door slams behind you. It's pitch-black.

Drip. Drip. Drip.

A spotlight shines on an urn hanging by a thread from the ceiling. You watch the pot slowly fill with water. When it completely fills, the string snaps, and the urn shatters on the ground. Oookayyyy. The room goes dark again, and you hear another sound.

Guuuuuusssssssshhhhhh.

The spotlight illuminates the opposite wall. Now, instead of one urn, there are seven. And instead of a drip, there's a steady stream. The water is filling the first pot, which is feeding into the next, and so on. You stare at the urns, waiting for them to start shattering. What a weird game. Eventually, something catches your attention below the pots. Looks like some sort of pedestal with seven spots.

The game must want you to arrange the urns on the pedestal to unlock the next room.

Creeeaaaaak.

Your eyes get wide when you realize that one of the urns is about to go down. If it shatters, you'll be trapped!

Find the urn that will fill with water first.
Turn to that urn's page number to see if you were right.

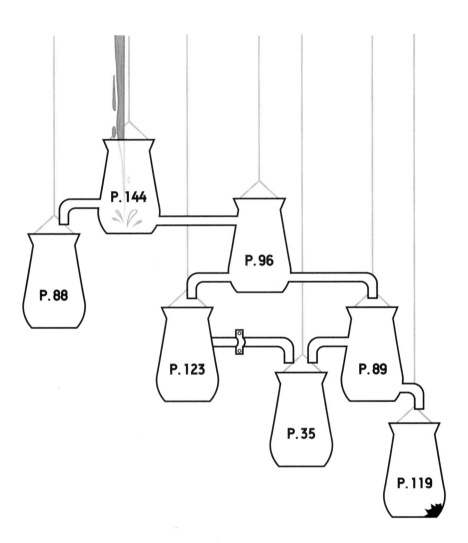

YOU'VE HEARD THAT snakes are especially sensitive in their nose, so you wind up for a punch. Actually, now that you think about it, you're not sure if that nose thing is true for snakes or sharks. Anyway, no time to second-guess yourself! Time to punch! Let's go! Punch! OK, now! Punch!

For some reason, you can't move your fist. It feels really heavy. In fact, your whole body feels heavy. The snake starts swaying. You start swaying. Its eyes are doing that weird spinning hypnosis thing that only happens in cartoons and video games. You let go of all your worry and start wondering what it'd be like to sleep inside a snake's belly. It's probably warm in there. Like a big sleeping bag.

The snake opens its mouth to invite you in. You thought it'd never ask.

A   ❗ ACHIEVEMENT UNLOCKED
SNAKE SLEEPOVER
RETURN TO CHECKPOINT ON P. 70

YOU CRAWL INTO the living quarters and lie low. No monster sounds for now. You take a breath and look around the room. In addition to the bunk beds, there's foosball, air hockey, and a *Pong* arcade machine. This would be a fun place to hang out if someone hadn't punched a hole in the *Pong* machine. And broken the air hockey table in half. And shoved foosball sticks through the walls.

You hear snorting behind you and dive under one of the bunk beds. It's a tight squeeze. You stop breathing when you hear sniffing. Wait, how good is this creature's sense of smell? You need to get out now. Doors leading to the main lab and kitchen are behind you. If you keep crawling forward, you should be able to sneak into the locker room. Underneath a bed to your left is a hole in the floor with a blue vine growing through it. You could use it to crawl down to the lower level.

SELECT

85 Kitchen.

78 Lab.

92 Locker room.

74 Blue vine.

YOU ROLL INTO the cave just as the vine speeds past. Whew, that was close. Wait a second—you don't hear the vine moving anymore. Does it know you're in the cave? You retreat deeper into the tunnel, then round a corner. It's pitch-black now, so you unclip your flashlight. Looks like there's a fork. You turn right. A few more steps, and the path splits into three branches. You take the one on the left. Now, there's a tunnel going up and a tunnel going down. You pause and consider whether you should continue. That's when you hear two sounds at the same time:

Sssssshhhhhh. Something's slithering behind you.

Sccccrrrrrrtch. Something's scratching the rocks below you.

You glance at the top tunnel. There's an orange glow. Looks like one of Shandling's edenberries. In the bottom tunnel, red eyes appear. Maybe a wolf? Just then, the vine appears behind you. You grip your grenade launcher. How do you want to handle this?

SELECT

15 Grenade.

62 Edenberry.

ONCE YOU REACH the kitchen, you have to silence a gag. The smell in here is a disgusting combination of sweet and rotten. You start working your way around the kitchen, looking for clues. On the counter, you see recipes scattered for pies, juices, jams, and all sorts of berry-related food. These researchers must have been putting edenberries into everything.

You duck when you hear a clank. The monster has arrived. You look into the reflection of a stainless steel dishwasher and see the creature headed your way. You scurry around a counter, then peek to see what your options are. There's flickering light behind a doorway covered in caution tape. There's a staircase lit by an orange glow next to the refrigerator. Finally, across the room, you find doorways to the living quarters and main lab. Where do you go?

SELECT

28 Flickering light.

94 Orange glow.

83 Living quarters.

78 Lab.

GO, GO, GO! You turn toward the hallway, but step on a stapler.

KACHUNK.

You freeze.

"GROWWWWWWL!"

You sprint into the hallway and round a corner. You have a few steps on the monster, which means you probably have time to hide inside one of these offices until it gives up the chase. You try the first office you see. Locked. You try the second. Locked. There's clanging behind you. You round a corner and almost crash into a door that's so mangled that it wouldn't open even if it were unlocked. You shine your flashlight at the ceiling as you run. Maybe you can swing into the ceiling tiles and . . .

"GROWL!"

This time, the sound is in front of you. You slam on the brakes just in time to avoid running into a second monster. When Monster #2 sees you, it sneers such an evil sneer that its face curls up like the Grinch.

❶ ACHIEVEMENT UNLOCKED
YOU'RE A MEAN ONE, MR. GRINCH
RETURN TO CHECKPOINT ON P. 78

TO SAY THE steroid piranhas hate you is an understatement. They hate you so much that they flop onto dry land and snarl gross, phlegmy snarls. You pick up the berry and notice it feels all tingly, like it's both hot and cold at the same time.

As soon as you eat the berry, time slows down. Cool! It's a power-up! Unfortunately, you slowed time just as one of the fish coughed, so you're stuck listening to "Haaaaaaaggggggk-krrrrllllllg." When you look at the fish, you're surprised that you somehow know everything about it. You know how fast it swims, how high it jumps, and how well it floats. This berry must be a superpower for your brain too!

Your superpowered brain uses this information to assemble a plan. Before you know what's happening, you find yourself grabbing the fish's tongue and throwing it toward its friends. Those fish jump out of the water to eat their pal, and you use them to bounce over to the next group of piranhas. Your new superhuman speed lets you turn the rest of the deadly piranhas into floating platforms that allow you to hop all the way down the river. You don't exactly know where you're going, but you'll trust your berry brain to figure it out.

TURN TO

P. 50

! ACHIEVEMENT UNLOCKED
PIRANHA PLATFORMING

PAGE THROUGH THE nearest thesaurus until . . . Yeah, a thesaurus. It's a big book of synonyms. Um, synonyms are words that mean the same thing. Anyway . . .

Really? You don't have a thesaurus? Ung.

OK, visit your local library, and . . . What do you mean you don't own a library card?! They're free! OK, find your birth certificate, go to your local library, and ask for a card. They should give you one as long as you also know your address and phone number. If you don't know those two things, memorize them right now because they're super important.

Once you have your library card, ask a librarian where the reference section is. Librarians are those people sitting behind the big desk who are silently begging you to ask a question. The librarian will take you to a thesaurus and ask if you know about the summer reading program. Say no even if you do, then listen politely while she explains the overly complicated game. When she finally leaves, page through the thesaurus until you find the word "foolish." Read all of the synonyms, knowing that each one describes the decision that brought you to this page.

T ❗ ACHIEVEMENT UNLOCKED
HAREBRAINED, INJUDICIOUS, AND DAFT
RETURN TO CHECKPOINT ON P. 113

FORTY THOUGHTS GO through your mind in the half-second between the moment you realize you've made the wrong choice and the moment you actually die. Those thoughts include:

How do eyebrows know when to stop growing?

Do fish pee?

Why don't sumo wrestlers become hockey goalies?

Where in the world is Carmen Sandiego?

Why does grape candy taste nothing like actual grapes?

Why doesn't glue stick to the inside of the bottle?

At what temperature does a Hot Pocket become a regular pocket?

Why does orange juice taste so bad after you brush your teeth?

Why don't psychics ever win the lottery?

Why can little kids make new teeth but adults can't?

If Cinderella's shoe fit so great, why did it fall off in the first place?

W ❗ ACHIEVEMENT UNLOCKED

GREAT QUESTIONS

RETURN TO CHECKPOINT ON P. 113

YOU HOLD OFF until the goop nearly reaches you, then take a deep breath and fire.

THUNK! PLOOMP!

The grenade gets stuck in the purple goop. Now what?

BOOM!

When the grenade explodes, the plant transforms into a cannon that shoots you across the treetop. You tuck in your legs as you fly through the air.

THUNK!

You land in another monster plant. This one is waving left and right. You pry it open just enough to see that when the plant is pointing right, it's facing a third Venus flytrap. When it's pointing left, it's facing the bee swarm. You time your grenade so you can shoot to the third plant. That one is spinning in a circle. You continue cannoning your way across the tree, always staying one step ahead of the bees.

The final plant is enormous. When you poke your head out, you notice that it's pointing at a glowing green statue of . . . is that a lime? Must be where you need to go. This plant is so large that it's filling much slower than the rest, which gives the bees time to catch up. When the glowing, purple goop is high enough, you pump three grenades into it and wait.

KABOOM!

You fly all the way to the final platform and tumble to a stop right in front of the fruit statue. You dust yourself off and reach for the fruit, but just before you touch it, two giant talons descend from the sky and rip it away.

"Seriously?!" You look up. It's a monstrous prehistoric bird covered in half-feathers, half-scales. It screeches at you, then zooms high into the air. A quick look around reveals four options: you can climb to a giant nest above you, eat an edenberry growing near your feet, use an oversized leaf as a hang glider, or dive off the tree.

SELECT

42 Nest.

112 Edenberry.

95 Leaf.

122 Dive.

AS YOU GET closer, you hear water hitting a tile floor. You poke in your head and discover a shower room with one of the stalls running. Is someone else here? You don't want to alert the monster by calling out, so you shine your light under the curtain.

No feet. You throw the curtain back and see a vine growing from the drain with a tendril wrapped around the shower knob. It's watering itself. There's something creepy about that, which makes you instinctively take a step backward.

OOF! You slip on a puddle, causing your flashlight to hit the ground with a loud, echoing *CLANK*. You scramble to a shower stall and close the curtain just as the monster sprints into the room. It starts throwing open curtains. Looks like there are three avenues of escape, two of which are in this very stall. First, you notice an opening in the wall behind you just big enough for your body to fit through. Next, you see a hole in the floor with a yellow vine growing through it. Finally, you realize that you can make it to the living quarters if you time your escape while the monster has its back turned.

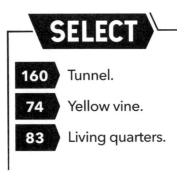

SELECT

160 Tunnel.

74 Yellow vine.

83 Living quarters.

AS SOON AS you pop the edenberry into your mouth, you realize that you don't even have to solve the puzzle. There's a secret stone halfway up the wall that you can push to reset the room. You push the button, and the stone flips over, revealing the blue idol. It has the number one carved into it. You smile when you pick it up. Aren't edenberries wonderful?

TURN TO
P.54

N ❗ ACHIEVEMENT UNLOCKED
EASIEST PUZZLE

AS YOU NEAR the room, the orange glow becomes so intense that it's almost overwhelming. You finally close your eyes and start navigating by feel.

SQUISH!

You open your eyes just enough to see that you've stepped on an edenberry that's 10 times bigger than any you've seen so far. You peer around the room as best you can. Looks like this is a growth lab where the experiment got out of control. Vines and berries have wrapped themselves around everything.

You quietly feel your way around the room. Around the first corner, the wall changes from tile to glass. A greenhouse, probably. You round the second corner and come upon a natural stone wall. A hole in this wall is blasting hot air like a furnace.

SQUISH! SQUISH! SQUISH!

Someone else is here! You could escape by climbing the stairs across the room or using a green vine to climb into the greenhouse. You could hide in the furnace tunnel. Or . . . you look at a ginormous edenberry at your feet. A brain boost might get you past this monster for good.

SELECT

- **85** Stairs.
- **74** Vine.
- **97** Tunnel.
- **49** Edenberry.

YOU PLUCK THE largest leaf you can find from the tree, hold it above your head, and jump. An updraft catches the leaf and rockets you into the air. You're actually flying! This is incredible. This must be how the Wright brothers felt. You ride the updraft all the way to the top of the tree, then look for the bird. Let's see, it was right—

RIIIIIIIP!

Uh-oh. The bird was above you the whole time, and it just slashed your fancy hang glider with its beak. You plummet to your death.

ACHIEVEMENT UNLOCKED
MORE LIKE THE WRONG BROTHERS
RETURN TO CHECKPOINT ON P. 90

WRONG. YOU'RE DEAD. This page will either help you feel better or kick you while you're down, depending on your attitude toward dad jokes.

What's the tallest building in any city?

The library. It has the most stories.

Why should you never let Elsa hold a baby?

She'll let it go.

Why don't you ever see elephants hiding in trees?

Because they're so good at it.

Why are crabs always backstabbing their friends?

They're shellfish.

What do you call a bear with no teeth?

A gummy bear.

Which birds are the best at building things?

Cranes.

What did the vegetarian zombie eat?

GRAAAAIIIIINS.

N > ❗ ACHIEVEMENT UNLOCKED
DAD! STOP!
RETURN TO CHECKPOINT ON P. 113

YOU WEDGE YOURSELF into the hole and hold still. Thirty silent seconds pass. Then—

"ROOOAAR!"

A big, furry hand smashes into the hole. You avoid it by lurching backward, but that causes you to tumble down a hidden vent. You bounce and roll until you land on your back in a boiling-hot cavern.

No way you can climb out of here. You're surrounded by smooth stone walls that rise up, up, up into a perfect circle above you. Suddenly, you realize where you are. It's a volcano! The earth rumbles, and you hop to your feet. The ground is cracked like it could crumble at any moment.

You assess your options. There's one small hole across the room. The last hole didn't work out great for you, but this one seems like your only real choice. On the other hand, maybe you're supposed to be in here for the explosion. It might even shoot you to safety. Where do you go?

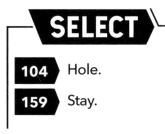

SELECT

104 Hole.

159 Stay.

YOU LOWER YOUR weapon when you see the monster's face. Its eyes are barely glowing. They're sad. They're pleading.

"I tried," the monster repeats. It's struggling to talk. "Please. Do. Not . . ." The monster winces with every word.

You wait while it catches its breath and notice something strange. Its orange fur is turning gray. Its grip on your ankle loosens. Its fingers wrinkle. Suddenly, you realize who this must be. "Shandling," you whisper.

By now, his hair is entirely gray, and he's shrunk to the size of an old man. "Stop him."

"But how?" you ask, even though you know Shandling can't hear you. He groans and closes his eyes.

"Bwahahahaha."

Declan's doing an evil villain laugh above you, and he sounds like a monster. You look up and notice a staircase in the shadows ahead.

Shandling looks at you again. "Now. Please."

"I can't!" you say. "Anything good I've done in this game has come from those dumb berries! Just tell me how to beat him. Can you do that, at least? Like, whatever it is probably won't work, but . . ."

You trail off when Shandling starts trembling. He's mustering all his strength to do something. You watch silently as he points to his eye with a shaky finger.

"Your eye? What about it?"

That's all Shandling's got. He lowers his finger and lies still. He's gone.

You gather enough courage to walk up the stairs. When you reach the top, you find yourself in a torchlit arena that's empty except for a chandelier of golden edenberries. Actually, "chandelier" makes it sound way nicer than it looks. It's more like a giant sac of spider eggs hanging from the ceiling by a tangle of vines. This must be the heart of the whole island. You raise your grenade launcher to take it out.

CRASH!

A giant orange monster drops in front of you. It looks like the monsters you encountered in the underground tunnels, but way bigger. Golden juice is dripping from its mouth. "Don't," it says in the strangest, deepest voice you've ever heard. Then it takes a step toward you and smiles a thin-lipped smile you've only seen one other place.

"Declan," you plead. "Please. I just want to get out of here."

"With this power, no one can stand in my way," the Declan monster says. "Especially you, Cooper Hawke."

You've got some ideas for standing in his way.

Pick three of the options below, then turn to the corresponding pages to learn how much damage you've dealt. If your three attacks total less than 100 HP, turn to p. 163. If they add up to 100 HP or more, turn to p. 153.

SELECT

- **103** Shoot Declan with a grenade.
- **105** Shoot the edenberries with a grenade.
- **107** Throw a torch at Declan.
- **110** Load a torch into your grenade launcher.
- **111** Light the room on fire.
- **117** Dodge Declan's attacks.

YOU CLIMB INTO the blue hole. It turns out to be a tunnel that's deeper than you thought. You keep climbing, but there's no end in sight. You finally decide to turn around. Unfortunately, the hole is too skinny for you to turn. You feel claustrophobic and start crawling backward. That's when you fall.

SQUISH!

You tumble into a pit filled with glowing blue mushrooms. The squished mushrooms transform into alien goo that starts climbing your leg. You shake your leg, but that just flings goo onto your arms. This could get messy.

L ❶ ACHIEVEMENT UNLOCKED

MUSHROOM KINGDOM

RETURN TO CHECKPOINT ON P. 131

AS SOON AS you clear the bridge, you drop a grenade behind you like you're playing *Mario Kart*.

BOOM!

Your grenade does its thing, and the bridge crumbles, taking Declan's truck with it.

"WOOOOHO—"

Your celebration is rudely cut short by Landra screaming at you. "YOU DINGUS!"

She's driving too fast to avoid the chasm. She turns the motorcycle into a skid, but it doesn't help. You both tumble down the pit.

❗ ACHIEVEMENT UNLOCKED
YOU DINGUS
RETURN TO CHECKPOINT ON P. 68

YOU AIM AT the middle of Declan's chest and squeeze the trigger. He's ready for it. You expected that. What you didn't expect was how fast he'd be able to throw it back. Declan catches the grenade, then winds up and throws a fastball at you. The best Major League pitchers can throw 100 mph. Declan throws this heater 250 mph. You have no chance to catch it.

KABOOM!

DAMAGE TO DECLAN: 0 HP

TURN TO

P. 100

YOU CHOOSE THE HOLE. How much worse could it be than the situation you're in now?

Guess what? It's worse. So. Much. Worse.

The hole leads to a tube that twists you around a few times before plopping you unceremoniously into a dark room. You brace yourself for a hard landing. Instead, something soft and squishy breaks your fall. You're thankful for the squishiness until you reach down and grab a fistful of fur. Uh-oh.

"GRRRRRRRRR."

A pair of glowing orange eyes reveal themselves. Then a second pair. And a third. You've just interrupted naptime at monster headquarters. That's not going to go over well.

E ❗ ACHIEVEMENT UNLOCKED
KILL THE ALARM CLOCK
RETURN TO CHECKPOINT ON P. 78

SEEMS LIKE DECLAN is pretty infatuated with those eden-berries. Let's see what happens if you take them out. You aim at the vines holding the berry chandelier and squeeze the trigger. Declan's eyes grow wide, and he jumps. The edenberry chandelier is at least 50 feet in the air. There's no way he can jump that high, right?

Wrong.

At the top of his jump, Declan stretches like an outfielder trying to keep a home run from clearing the fence. The grenade lands in his big paw, and he clenches it tight.

BOOM!

When Declan hits the ground again, he's furious. He screams at the ceiling, looks at his smoking hand, then throws a monster temper tantrum. You raise your grenade launcher, but Declan doesn't let you fire another shot. He balls up his fists and hits the ground so hard that you fall backward and drop your weapon.

DAMAGE TO DECLAN: 30 HP

TURN TO

P. 100

ONCE YOU GET inside the tunnel, you gasp. That bright light you saw was coming from the sun. Like, the actual sun. You're standing on a beautiful beach next to a waterfall hundreds of feet underground, and the sun is somehow shining at full intensity. Is this like *Journey to the Center of the Earth* where you get to dinosaur land once you reach the middle of the earth?

You bend over to pick up a handful of sand, but it goes right through your fingers. Not because it's so fine, but because it doesn't exist. You reach down again. Weird. It looks like you're touching sand, but all you feel is stone. You step toward the waterfall, and the ground suddenly disappears under your feet.

Only when you fall through the island do you see what's really going on. This cavern is lined with a ring of plants that are projecting a hologram into the room. All the plants look like they're connected by vines to something at the bottom of the pit. But what is . . .

CHOMP!

It's a monster mirage plant with teeth.

❗ ACHIEVEMENT UNLOCKED

PHANTOM PHANTOM ISLAND

RETURN TO CHECKPOINT ON P. 159

YOU GRAB A torch from the wall and run toward Declan, screaming. The monster smiles in amusement. You wish you had more of a plan, but this is the best you've got. When you get within throwing distance of the monster, you whip the torch at Declan's face.

Instead of dodging the torch, Declan's eyes flash, and he freezes for a second. That hesitation provides just enough time for the torch to hit his face and singe some hair.

Declan smacks his face to put out the fire, grits his teeth, and growls.

DAMAGE TO DECLAN: 20 HP

TURN TO

P. 100

YOU SPREAD YOUR arms and bank hard right, hoping you can steer just enough to land on the roof.

WOOMF!

Success! You tumble into a second-story bedroom, then pop up and sprint downstairs. Maybe you can wait out the bees down here.

Bzzzzzzzzz.

They're coming. You lean against the door and try to quiet your breathing. After a minute, the buzzing stops. Did they move on? You look through the keyhole, then put a hand over your mouth to stifle a scream. A bee is crawling through. You run to the other side of the room and pull out your grenade launcher as a warning. The bee emerges from the keyhole and practically laughs at you. Both of you know that a grenade's not going to do anything against a giant swarm. You watch helplessly as more bees crawl through the hole, then clump together to form a hand that slowly turns the doorknob. Finally, they throw open the door to welcome the mob.

⚠ ACHIEVEMENT UNLOCKED

WELCOME HOME

RETURN TO CHECKPOINT ON P. 59

YOU PUT THE final symbol in place just as the room fills with water. The stone flips, and you dive down to collect the idol. When you do, you see a scrap of paper floating toward you. Since it's not glowing, you assume it's unimportant and keep swimming. However, at the last second, two words scrawled on the note catch your attention: "video game."

If you're reading this, you are trapped inside *The Secret of Phantom Island*. You need to know that the video game isn't what it seems, and the way out isn't what you think. I can tell you how to get out, but not here. It's not safe. Look for my first clue on the copyright page (that's the boring page with tiny print at the very beginning of the book). After you read the note, return to this page, and proceed like normal. They can't know that you know!

You're more confused than ever after reading the note. You dive down and pick up the idol. It has the number one carved into it. Everything disappears, and you find yourself back in front of the tree.

TURN TO

P.54

❗ ACHIEVEMENT UNLOCKED

SECRET NOTE

YOU GRAB A torch from the wall and try shoving it into your grenade launcher. This probably won't work—you don't think anyone has ever really tried launching anything besides grenades out of a grenade launcher because grenades are usually more than enough to do the job. It takes longer than you'd like to load the torch because Declan is throwing things at you, and also there's the small detail of the torch being on fire. Once you finally get the torch stuffed into your launcher, you aim at Declan's face and squeeze the trigger.

"ARRRRRRRRRGH!"

The torch's light freezes Declan in place so he can't dodge, and the projectile hits him in the forehead. The fire burns Declan's hair in a pattern that looks kind of like confused eyebrows. Declan grabs more berries, grows even bigger, then launches an angrier attack. You've found something, though. Edenberry monsters seem to be affected by flashes of light. You launch three more successful attacks with your homemade torch launcher before running out of torches.

DAMAGE TO DECLAN: 50 HP

TURN TO

P. 100

DECLAN IS SO much bigger, faster, stronger, and smarter than you that there's no way you can beat him by yourself. You look for help from your environment. You've got the edenberry chandelier above you, torches all around you, and that's pretty much it. Oh, and spiderwebs are covering all the walls. Is that something?

Maybe it is. You dodge a Declan attack, grab a torch, then light one of the webs. *WHOOSH!* Fire spreads across the webs, heating the room 100 degrees in a second. The sudden flash sends Declan stumbling around, shielding his eyes from the light. This gives you the perfect opportunity to launch a grenade.

Good news: You land a direct hit. Bad news: Your hit snaps Declan out of it. Declan pounds the ground, sending a shockwave that throws you back into the fire. You stop, drop, and roll, just like you learned in your field trip to the fire station, then stand back up and square your shoulders. Let's go, orange monster.

DAMAGE TO DECLAN: 30 HP

TURN TO

P. 100

YOU KNOW YOU shouldn't eat the berry until you learn more about it, but if you ever needed a power-up, this seems like the time. You pop the berry into your mouth, and a headache you didn't know you had suddenly clears. You now understand the meaning of life, the universe, and everything. It's 42.

A path up the tree reveals itself, and you start climbing like a monkey. Soon, you're climbing faster than the bird can fly. As soon as you're above the bird, you jump on top of it, grab its head, and start steering. You fly through the tree canopy while cackling maniacally. After a while, your brain starts feeling foggy again, so you dive down for a landing.

By the time you touch down, your head is way foggier than it was before, and your stomach feels upset. You hear a deep, rumbling laugh. Did that come from you? The bird is gone, and you somehow have the green statue in your hands. It's displaying the number two. The world fades, and you return to the clearing.

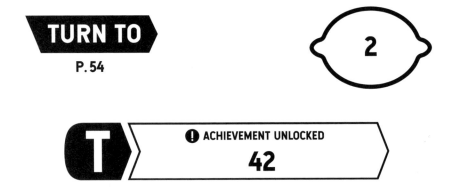

TURN TO

P. 54

2

❗ ACHIEVEMENT UNLOCKED

42

YOU STEP ONTO the blue section of the circle, and it clicks like a button. The earth begins rumbling—gently at first, then so hard that it knocks you down. Eventually, the ground splits open to reveal an enormous pit in front of you. When the rumbling finally stops, you scoot to the edge of the hole and peer down. Then, you almost fall into the hole when the shaking starts again. You probably should have fallen, but a miracle gust of wind kept you upright. You scramble back and watch a building emerge from the hole.

The building looks like something that should be called a "Temple of Doom." It's a centuries-old stone structure with scary statues all over it. Oh, and its main entrance is a 50-foot skull. When the temple finally finishes rising, you creep to the door and lay a hand on it. Something clicks inside the temple, the skull starts humming, and the jaw slowly lowers so you can enter.

Creeeeeepy.

You grit your teeth and walk inside. It doesn't look that big. Maybe the size of a living room or . . .

CRASH!

The jaw slams shut behind you. Then more rumbling, and the room's stone floor transforms into stairs that lead to a glowing lower level. Terrific. You step onto the first stair.

Click.

A light turns on. You look around for a moment before testing the second step.

Click.

Something whirs deep inside the temple. Each additional step clicks another process into motion. Third step: the ceiling opens to reveal a system of gears, sprockets, and chains. Fourth step: the ceiling machinery starts moving. Fifth step: steam fills the staircase. By the time you reach the bottom of the stairs, the temple is practically shaking from all the activity. There's a boulder rumbling through an oversized marble track, a turbine powered by an underground waterfall, and about a million whirring wheels, blades, and drills that don't appear to actually serve a purpose. You stare at the spectacle for a long time before you notice a glowing piece of paper at your feet. Looks like another Shandling entry.

May 25, 1975

The lost temple stands as a testament to the grand potential that lies within us all if only we allow the edenberry to unlock it. The structure appears to have been built hundreds, if not thousands, of years ago, yet it is powered by electricity. Electricity! Who would have thought the first humans to harness electricity lived on a Pacific island centuries before Edison was born?

In addition to its achievements, this temple is loaded with danger. Its builders have protected its treasure well. Only those who demonstrate an intellect matching that of the natives can survive. Fortunately, the edenberries have proven up to the task. I believe we will crack the final code tomorrow.

One final thought enters my head before I slumber tonight. I wonder what became of the people who lived here. It is a shame that they never made it off the island.

—William K. Shandling

After you finish the note, you start looking for a way out of this room. It takes you a few minutes because there's so much going on, but it looks like the game wants you to either push or pull a handle. Before you grab the handle, you study the web of gears it powers. If you choose the correct direction, a rock will open the door in front of you. If you pick the wrong direction, you'll take an anvil to the head. No pressure.

SELECT

144 Push forward.

47 Pull backward.

DECLAN HAS LEARNED a number of attacks, including:

GROUND POUND. He smashes the ground so hard that shockwaves roll across the arena. These waves will knock you down if you don't jump over them.

JUMP AND SMASH. Declan is incredibly athletic for such a big monster. He keeps finding better angles to launch his attacks by jumping high into the air and kicking off the walls.

THROWING THINGS. Every once in a while, Declan will rip off a chunk of the wall and throw it at you just for fun.

OLD-FASHIONED HAYMAKER. A big ol' punch in the nose.

You find that you can dodge most of these attacks by jumping, ducking, and rolling. Unfortunately, that only works for so long. Declan keeps growing bigger and stronger by popping more edenberries into his mouth. You get tiny windows here and there to land attacks of your own, but you'll need more if you want to take him down.

DAMAGE TO DECLAN: 10 HP

TURN TO

P. 100

TURN TO P. 100

YOU'VE FELT STRANGE after every berry you've consumed, but this one is different. It fills you with such energy that you could explode. You take a deep breath to steady yourself, then look at the wires. They all appear to be perfectly straight. As you reach toward the first wire, your vision turns fuzzy. You blink and hold your hands to your face. Wait, your vision's not fuzzy, your hands are! They're covered in orange fur. You desperately grab for a wire, but your hands are too chunky to grip it. Are you . . .

"MONSTER!"

You spin around. Declan is pointing his gun at you and backing up in horror. Your heart sinks, but you smile an evil Grinchy grin anyway. You'll never beat the game like this, but you can at least beat up Declan.

L ❗ ACHIEVEMENT UNLOCKED

WHO'S THE MONSTER NOW?

RETURN TO CHECKPOINT ON P. 132

THIS IS THE wrong choice. You die. The death is so agonizing that it can only be described as an acrostic. What's an acrostic, you ask? Pay attention to the first letter of each line below, and you'll understand.

Horrible
Aaarrrgblbl
Woof, that was bad
Kinda worse than you thought
Eek

Don't look
Everything is awful
Aaarrrgblbl again
Dead

❗ ACHIEVEMENT UNLOCKED

AAARRRGBLBL

RETURN TO CHECKPOINT ON P. 113

THIS TIME WHEN the cannon shoots you down the hallway, you don't get a chance to study the carving. You only catch a quick glimpse before falling into the key room.

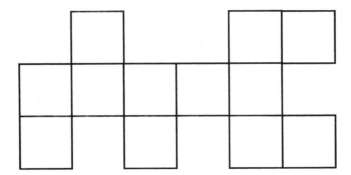

The key room is now filled almost entirely with water. The keys are all floating, and you've got to dive to get a good look.

Find the 3D key on the next page that matches the 2D side view above. You must hold your breath to look at the keys on this page. If you need to get air, you can look up and take a breath; however, you must rotate the book before you look back down.

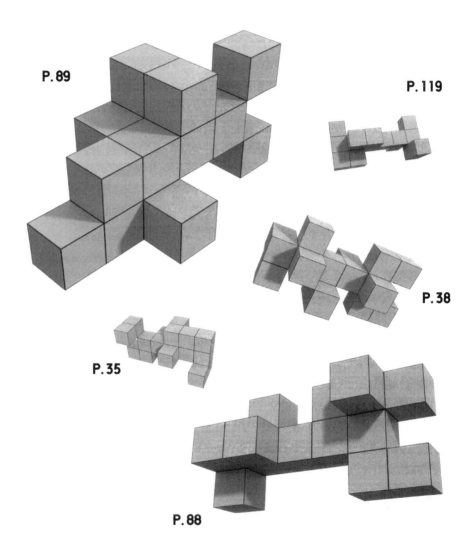

P.89

P.119

P.38

P.35

P.88

YOU JUMP OFF the platform for one of two reasons:

1. You remember the carving you saw was shaped like a big "down" arrow.

2. You are a lunatic.

You fall for 12 seconds, which, in falling time, equates to 12 hours. That's enough time to realize maybe that wasn't a picture of an arrow after all. Maybe it was an upside-down house. How silly to—

THOONK!

You land in the mouth of one of those purple monster plants. Never a doubt! You wait for the plant to fill with goop, then shoot a grenade.

BOOM!

You rocket into the air, which surprises the bird. It tries to swerve out of the way, but it's too late. You reach out and touch the glowing lime statue with your fingertips. You feel dizzy. The last thing you see before blacking out and returning to the clearing is a number glowing on the lime. It's two.

TURN TO

P. 54

2

❗ ACHIEVEMENT UNLOCKED

DOWN IS THE NEW UP

YOU LUNGE FOR the urn just as it begins to fall. After you make sure it's safe, you return to carefully remove the other six. Once you set them all on the ground, you notice that each urn has a letter carved into its base. You then take a closer look at the pedestal. There's an inscription.

We are small, but we are mighty

In the darkness, we shine brightly

Not straw, not blue,

But something new.

Eat us up,

We're good for you.

You stare at the letters for a moment, then re-read the poem. You have no idea. Suddenly, a voice pops into your head. Your own voice. It's saying the letter *B*. You place *B* on the first pedestal and try to figure out the rest of the word.

> *You'll notice some of the letters have numbers underneath. Once you unscramble the word, the three numerals will come together to form a three-digit number. That's the page you need to turn to next. The correct page will start with the phrase, "When you unscramble."*

TURN TO P. _1_ __ __

YOU BREATHE A sigh of relief when you cut the last wire. You can now add "bomb defuser" to your resume.

"Impressive."

You spin around. Declan is approaching with his arms wide open for a hug. You rear back to punch him, but he's quick to draw his knife.

"Friends, remember? I think you forgot that earlier when you ran off, but it's OK. I did a bit of surgery while you were sleeping." He pats the back of his head.

You rub your head and feel a bump that you'd assumed had come from one of your many misadventures. You realize now that it's an implanted tracking device.

"Now that my plane's destroyed, might as well get cozy." Declan sits down criss-cross applesauce. "Why don't you tell me what you've learned, Hawke? What is the secret of Phantom Island?"

Hawke? Oh, right, you forgot that Declan is reciting lines and doesn't realize who you really are. As long as he can't understand you, might as well roast him with one more sick burn. "It's that you're _____."

Insert sick burn.

Declan casually picks one of the golden berries. "No rush. We're going to be here for a while."

You lunge for the berry. "NO!"

Too late. Declan pops it into his mouth before you can reach him. His eyes immediately widen and glow orange. You can see his mind processing a billion pieces of information all at once.

He reaches back down, grabs a handful of berries, and pops them all into his mouth. His skin turns bright orange, and he springs to his feet.

"Listen. Declan. There's something . . ."

Declan shoves you out of the way, punches through the barrels, and sprints deeper into the great tree. Stop him! You give chase, but he's already gone. Scrambling and scraping noises from above tell you that you need to figure out a way up this tree if you want to reach him. You squint into the darkness but can't see much since the only light is coming from flickering torches. Wait, who lit these torches? Is this an unrealistic video game thing, or is someone else in here?

You step forward and find that the floor is springy. Looks like you're standing on a giant spiderweb. "Gross!" You jump backward and bump your head on a boulder. Actually, it looks like you might be able to climb the boulder. Once you pull yourself up, you find that it leads to a ledge, which you can use to jump to an even higher ledge. You jump and climb the ledges lining the tree until there's nowhere else to go except for one final platform all the way across the tree.

Your best option for getting over there appears to be a vine hanging from the ceiling. You could also try a leap of faith. While you decide, something above you screams a gurgled cry for help. Hurry up!

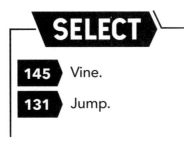

SELECT

145 Vine.

131 Jump.

EVEN THOUGH YOU'D love to escape the video game, it just doesn't seem right to destroy humanity in the process. So instead of grabbing the berries, you punch your clone in the face. Wow. That felt great. So great that you're surprised people don't punch you in the face more often.

"So that's the way it's going to be?" your clone asks. You nod. It is the way it's going to be. The clone points to the door, and it disappears. You quietly gulp and reach into your pocket in case grenades magically appeared. No grenades, but you do find a note that hadn't been there before.

I hope you found my first note. If you did, please turn to the section I mentioned in that note and read the first word of each page. When you put those four words together, you'll find your next instructions.

> *Choose two of the four options below to attack your clone.*
> *You'll succeed if you deal over 100 HP of damage.*

SELECT

127 Shove the berry into your clone's mouth.

128 Shine a flashlight at your clone's eyes.

129 Find a weak spot on your clone's back.

130 Show your clone a mirror.

YOU WIND UP like you're going to throw a punch, which causes your clone to get into a defensive stance with its arm in front of its face. Perfect. Instead of throwing a punch, you whack the clone's hand so the berry flies into its mouth. The clone chokes for a second.

"How about that for a taste of your own medicine?!" you taunt loudly and foolishly. Those are your last words before the clone transforms into an enormous monster and squishes you.

DAMAGE DEALT: 0 HP

TURN TO

P. 126

BLINDING LIGHT WORKED on the Declan monster, right? Maybe it'll work on this new threat too. You whip your flashlight out of your belt and shine it directly into your clone's eyes. The eyes don't even blink. If anything, they look confused.

You start to panic. Is there a switch to make the light brighter? Maybe if you bounce the light off a mirror? Nope, that doesn't work. Maybe if you . . .

Your clone snatches the flashlight out of your hand and clobbers you over the head with it.

DAMAGE DEALT: 0 HP

TURN TO

P. 126

YOU PRETEND TO stare at your clone to hide your interest in the opportunity you just spotted in a mirror across the room.

"What are you staring at?" your clone demands.

"Nothing!" But it is something. The clone has a small, glowing bump on the back of its head. That must be its weak spot.

"No, seriously. What are you looking at?"

"Nothing!" You don't want to blow this chance.

"Is it behind me?!" Your clone turns all the way around, exposing its back to you. There it is! Hit it now! You karate chop the spot as hard as you can. The clone, unfortunately, does not self-destruct. Instead, it turns and smiles. "You thought that was a weak spot, didn't you?"

"Huh? No, I . . ."

"You have one too. It's the tracking device Declan put in your head. See?" With that, your clone knocks you out with a single hit.

DAMAGE DEALT: 0 HP

P. 126

YOUR CLONE IS just artificial intelligence, right? Well, what if you showed it its own reflection in the mirror? Couldn't that short-circuit its brain? You don't know too much about artificial intelligence, but that seems right from everything you've seen in movies. You kick one of the mirrors out of the wall, flip it in your hand, then point it at your clone all in one motion.

Your clone reaches out, but stops when it sees its reflection. Its mouth starts to twitch. Promising! You hold the mirror closer.

"Bwahahahaha!" the clone breaks down in uncontrolled laughter. "Do you want to walk me through your thought process there? You thought a mirror would melt my brain or something? Look around you! This whole room is literally a mirror!"

Well, now you feel a little silly, don't you?

DAMAGE DEALT: 0 HP

TURN TO

P. 126

Hint: Did you complete the puzzle at the end of the temple on page 39? If you used the edenberry to skip it, you may want to go back and finish it. You just might uncover something useful if you do.

YOU SWING YOUR arms and jump as far as you can. Of course, you don't make it across the tree. Not even close. You barely make it to the edge of the spider's web. Fortunately, that's enough. Once you hit the web, you trampoline high into the air. On the second bounce, you time a jump for maximum height. On the third bounce, you get your arms into it. Sixteen more hops finally get you to the ledge.

Once you reach the ledge, you discover that you need to climb straight up with barely anything to grip. You sigh and start climbing. Halfway up the wall, your fingers feel like they're about to fall off, but you keep climbing for two reasons: Declan's cackle above and the long fall below.

Finally, you reach a narrow ledge and catch your breath. Up here, there are no more torches to guide you. The only light is a faint glow coming from two holes. The hole on your right is glowing purple. The hole on your left is glowing blue. There doesn't appear to be anywhere else for you to go. Which hole do you choose?

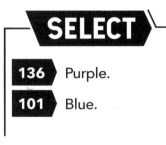

SELECT

136 Purple.

101 Blue.

WHEN YOU SET the final fruit in its place, the stone glows, the earth rumbles, and the tree door begins sliding open. Suddenly— *CRUNCH!*—the door stops moving. You inspect it closer. Looks like someone used a chain to keep it closed. You look for something you can use to cut the chain and notice a glowing piece of paper just inside the door. More Shandling.

You drop the paper after you finish reading. What now? The tree starts groaning like it's working really hard to open the door, then—*SNAP!*—the chain breaks.

When you look inside the tree, your palms get sweaty, you stumble backward, and you let out an involuntary scream. Here's why:

SWEAT. A whole patch of super edenberries are growing in here. You know they're super because they're gold instead of orange.

STUMBLE. Someone used red spray paint to scrawl a message inside the tree: "GET OUT."

SCREAM. Your path is blocked by a tower of barrels all connected to a digital timer by a tangle of wires. The timer currently reads 5:00. It is, without a doubt, a bomb.

You can't let this tree blow up! It's your only hope of beating the game and getting back to the real world!

Nnnnnroooooooooom!

You hear a plane overhead. Someone's coming to rescue you! You look up, and your heart sinks. It's a small black jet that you'd recognize anywhere. Declan. He must have followed you. He's flying low, looking for a runway. Fortunately, there's no . . .

THWIP!

June 2, 1975

I was wrong. About everything. This island must remain hidden for the rest of time. Its great tree must remain sealed, for it contains both unthinkable power and unspeakable evil. Its berries have ruined my men. They have ruined my brain. I suspect they have ruined my new pet, Ringo, although I cannot be sure because I have not seen him in several days. If someone does stumble upon this island, I have taken steps to ensure the destruction of the tree. I have also—

I hear something. The ground is shaking. Is my feeble mind playing tricks on me again? Oh no. It cannot be! A beast the size of an elephant is stalking me. Its tangled orange fur and glowing eyes make it look like a nightmare, but its long stripe gives it away. Ringo has been transformed. I must leave now. I cannot die, for the duty falls upon me to protect future explorers from the horrors that lie within the great tree.

—William K. Shandling

A giant vine reaches into the sky, snatches the plane like it's a toy, then pulls it down to the island. Great. If a bomb weren't bad enough, now Declan's here too. You turn your attention back to the wires. You've never defused a bomb before, but you've seen plenty of movies where people do. You've just got to untangle the wires to figure out which to cut first, second, and third. You look at the edenberries at your feet. Is this worth one more berry?

SELECT

118 Eat edenberry.

135 Defuse bomb.

If you choose to defuse the bomb, follow the wires from each number to the correct shape. Get all three correct, and you'll discover the page number you need to turn to next. There's only one correct solution, so if you end up on a page that doesn't make sense, come back and try again.

TURN TO P. ___ ___ ___

WHEN YOU CLIMB into the hole, you hear a gurgle, then a snap as large teeth close behind you. Purple goo starts pumping in. You grin when you recognize that goo. You've reached one of the flytrap cannon plants! You shoot a grenade into the goo and wait.

BOOM!

You fly across the tree into another cannon plant, then get shot into a third plant. You keep cannonballing until you reach a ledge at the very top of the tree. When you land on the ledge, you find a surprise that almost causes you to fall off. It's another monster.

You fumble with your grenade launcher but discover that there's no need. It's almost dead. The monster is wheezing on the ground, holding its side. You try creeping around it, but it snatches your leg. You fumble with your grenade launcher. If you play this right, you might still have time to take it out.

"I tried to stop him."

Wait, did the monster just talk? What do you do?

SELECT

55 Shoot the monster.

98 Listen to the monster.

THE SCREECHING STOPS once you start the machine. When you step through the door, a catapult scoops you into another cannon. You go through the same routine you remember from before—turn to the blade hallway, spear hallway, pit, then the clear hallway. You muster all your powers of concentration. Let's go.

From the clear hallway, the cannon moves two clicks right, then one left, three right, then four left.

It's moving faster than before, but you've been keeping track, and you know you're facing the clear hallway again. But then, the cannon throws a twist at you. A literal twist. It flips backward, so you're now facing the spear hallway upside down. When you're upside down, you have to remember that you're moving in the opposite direction. Right is actually left.

The turns come faster now. Right. Right. Left. Right three clicks. Left six clicks. Then you flip again. You're facing the opposite direction, and you're right side up again. Left two clicks. Right five clicks.

How do you get to the clear hallway?

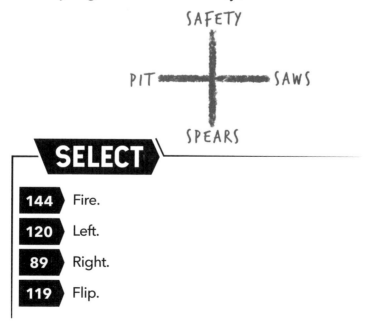

SELECT

144 Fire.

120 Left.

89 Right.

119 Flip.

ALTHOUGH DIVING INTO plants armed with teeth feels like it's probably the wrong choice, these guys look similar to the plant in the carving, so you take the chance. When you get closer, the plants sense a meal and grow big enough to swallow Cooper Hawke. They open up, showing off row after row of fangs. Too late to change course now. You close your eyes and land in the biggest plant. It chomps down and swallows you whole.

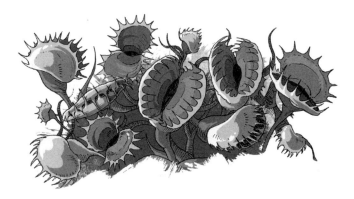

Now, here's a good news, bad news situation:

GOOD NEWS. You're safe from the bees!

BAD NEWS. You're about to find out how a carnivorous plant's digestive system works.

Glowing purple goop starts pumping into the plant. You bend over to touch the goop, then immediately pull your hand back. Acid! You inch your feet up the walls to stay ahead of the rising acid. When you reach the top of the plant, you have a decision to make. Are you going to open it and take your chances with the bees? Or are you going to fight back with your grenades?

SELECT

64 Bees.

90 Grenades.

YOU BLOW UP the barrier's base, which causes it to flip over into a perfect ramp instead of explode into pieces. It should be noted that this is a wonderful video game coincidence that has never once worked in real life. Landra guns the engine and flies over the chasm. You look back to see the headlights from Declan's truck go up the ramp, then point down over the cliff when the ramp cracks under the weight of his truck. The last thing you can make out in the darkness is Declan scrambling to safety before his truck plunges down the cliff.

Landra turns and winks at you, then everything goes black. "Wait, whaaaa . . ." you say while you blink a couple times. Just as quickly as the world disappeared, however, it reappears. Only now, you're not on a motorcycle. You're in a beautiful cliffside villa overlooking the ocean. You blink in confusion for a few seconds before you remember that you're in a video game, and video games always skip the boring parts of life. You rub the back of your head. You've got some bumps back there, but otherwise, everything seems OK. Landra's on the balcony, so you walk out to join her.

You stand next to Landra and look at the stars, trying not to peek at the impossibly tall woman standing next to you. You finally glance over and notice Landra's long, black hair is still perfectly styled, even after those last 15 minutes of insane driving. Standing awkwardly next to Landra, you feel very much like a little kid pretending to be an adult. You break the silence by clearing your throat. Landra doesn't acknowledge you. The game must want you to say something. "Uh, hey, Ms. Landra," you try. "Or, Ms. Lovodo, er, Lovato, I think? Anyway, I'm not sure if you can hear me, but I was hoping you could help me, like, get out of here."

Landra smirks. "I know you don't have the map." Your shoulders slump. She's playing a part just like Declan, which means she can't understand you either. Landra turns to you, and her eyes light up. "You know how I know that?" She unzips one of her jacket pockets and pulls out a brown, tattered pirate map–looking thing. "Because I found the map myself."

You stare at the map. Is this your ticket out of the game?

"I wasn't going to show you, but I can't figure out what it means," Landra continues. "Can you help me?"

The map is gibberish. Maybe you could figure it out if you were a world-class treasure hunter, but you can't even figure out those maps you're supposed to use to get around amusement parks. You try to change the subject by sharing an interesting fact you know about pirates. "Did you know that pirates _____?"

Insert pirate fact. It doesn't have to be true.

Landra glares at you like she hates pirates with the fury of a thousand suns. "What did you say?"

" _____."

Sheepishly repeat pirate fact.

"Destroy it. Really, Coop? You want me to destroy the map after all I went through to get it? Are you crazy?!"

Landra looks like she wants to punch you, so you back up a few steps. "No! No, no, no. It's your map! Do whatever you want with it!"

Landra's eyes are basically on fire now. "Yeah, Coop. I read the diary too. I know what happened to those guys. But since when do we worry about danger? We're treasure hunters! This is what we do!" She winds up like she actually might punch you.

You back up so fast that you trip over yourself. "I take back whatever you think I said!"

Landra stops herself from throwing a punch, then calmly says, "You can destroy the next treasure map you find, how about that? This one's mine." She stuffs the map back into her pocket and points to the door. "Now, get out of my house." With that, she turns and marches away.

As soon as Landra turns, you hear a whoosh, and time seems to slow. The map in her pocket is glowing. A meter appears in the corner of your vision below the words "pickpocket mode." Act quickly if you want that map. The meter is depleting fast.

> *To pick the map out of Landra's pocket without her noticing, grab only the next two pages using just the tips of your right thumb and index finger. You'll know if you succeeded if you see a map. If you turn more or fewer than two pages, you lose a life and must try again.*

WHEN YOU UNSCRAMBLE the word, the pedestal sinks into the ground, and the stream of water that had been filling the urns turns into a flood. A passageway opens across the room, and you run into a large cavern. In here, even more water is gushing. The whole temple seems to be flooding. There's an inscription to your right.

> *Be smart, be sure, be brave, be fast*
> *These 12 minutes may be your last.*

In front of you is a huge machine similar to the one you encountered at the beginning of the temple. Easy. You've got this.

> *You have 12 minutes to complete the temple. Start a timer now. If you don't finish in time, you lose a life and must restart from this point.*

But while you study the contraption, you're interrupted by an earsplitting screech. Where is that coming from?! You cover your ears, but the sound doesn't go away. It's so piercing that you can't think.

> *Combat the screech by humming the entire time you solve this puzzle. The more annoying the song, the better.*

SELECT

137 Lift up.

96 Push down.

THIS IS THE wrong choice. You die. That's all there is to it, but since it'd be a shame to waste the rest of this page, please enjoy this serious portrait of a bear who believes he is George Washington.

H

❗ ACHIEVEMENT UNLOCKED

GRIZZLY WASHINGTON

RETURN TO CHECKPOINT ON P. 113

AFTER EVERYTHING VINES have done to you on this island, you're really going to trust one now, huh? Well, let's see how this plays out.

You jump and reach for the vine. Predictably, you don't grab it. It grabs you. You kick and struggle, but the vine wraps your wrists tighter. Sigh. It's no use. Might as well enjoy the ride. The vine lowers you to the edge of the web, and a spider the size of a minivan crawls up. Its eight orange eyes stare at you. Now would be a good time to scream.

E ❗ ACHIEVEMENT UNLOCKED

SERIOUSLY. NEVER TRUST A VINE.

RETURN TO CHECKPOINT ON P. 124

YOU SNEAK OUT of Landra's house before opening the map. It's a cool map for sure, but not in a way that would be helpful for, like, going somewhere. If the artist had spent as much time labeling things as he did drawing sweet dragons in the ocean, this would be a lot more helpful. And what is "follow" supposed to mean anyway? You stare at the map until your vision starts to blur. Whoa! What was that?

When you stop focusing on the details of the map, you finally see the secret message it's hiding, and you know exactly what you're supposed to follow. What is it?

> *There's only one correct answer, so if the page you reach doesn't make sense, return here and try again.*

SELECT

10 Ship.

148 Monster.

66 Bird.

30 River.

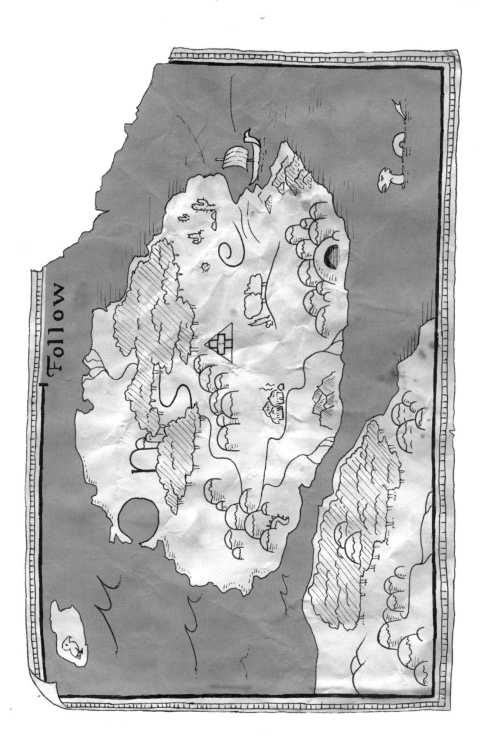

Follow

BRIGHT LIGHT SWALLOWS everything, and you find yourself back in the cube mirror room. A hand rests on your shoulder. When you turn to see who it is, the room blinks, then goes black.

"Who are you? What's going on?!" you yell.

"Find me," a voice whispers.

With that, you return to the video game. You're behind the wheel of a small boat in the middle of a giant nighttime storm. Waves are tossing you like crazy.

"Find you where?!" you shout as you struggle with the wheel. No answer. There was something about that whisper. Something familiar. You play it back in your mind, then jump out of your skin when you hear a telephone ring.

You look to your left. It's one of those big satellite phones that you have to use when you're climbing mountains or approaching uncharted islands. You pick it up and repeat your question. "Find you where?!"

"COOPER JAMES HAWKE, YOU'D BETTER NOT BE WHERE I THINK YOU ARE!"

Ung. Landra. "Listen," you try. "I'm not even sure how I got here. Also, do you know anything about a mirror room with . . ."

"AFTER ALL I DID FOR YOU, YOU GO WITHOUT ME?!"

"I promise that I did not mean to leave without you, OK? I don't even know how to steer a boat! You seem like someone who knows how to steer a boat."

"I SWEAR, WHEN I FIND YOU, I WILL KILL YOU. DO YOU HEAR ME?! I WILL . . ."

Thwack.

The phone gets slapped out of your hand.

You spin around. "Who's that?!" The cabin is dark except for a dim red glow cast by some of the instruments. The only noise is wind whistling through an open window. You slam the window closed and start breathing faster. That slap was all wet and slippery and definitely not human. Maybe a fish flopped through the window? You decide to stick with that theory while you look for a weapon. Oh, good. There's your trusty grenade launcher behind you. You pick it up and peer around the cabin before creeping to the back of the boat.

Once you get outside, rain pelts your face. You try again. "Hello?"

Howling wind is your only answer. You squint into the darkness. You can't make out anything, except . . . Is that a pole sticking out of the ocean? You fumble with your utility belt and find a flashlight. You turn it on just in time to glimpse something disappear below the waves.

Not good. Noooooooot good. You run back inside, slam the door, and start hitting every button and switch in sight. This boat has got to have lights somewhere. You finally flip a switch that causes a spotlight on top of the boat to flicker. You freeze. Your boat just happens to be cresting a wave when the light comes on, which gives you a perfect view of the horror below. Five tentacles, each at least 50 feet tall, are waving back and forth, waiting to destroy you.

"KRAAAAAAKEN!" you scream as you open the window and aim your grenade launcher. You've seen krakens in pirate movies, and you know they're nothing to fool around with. You're not sure if your tiny grenades are capable of taking down a giant squid from the deep, but you're not going down without finding out.

THUNK. BOOM!

You score a direct hit on one of the tentacles with your first shot. You hear a screech, then the tentacle disappears underwater. The remaining four start speeding toward you.

THUNK. BOOM! SCREECH!

Two down, but the rest are moving faster than ever. You load another grenade, then feel yourself go weightless. The kraken has tossed your boat into the air. A second later, you crash sideways into the ocean. As water starts pouring into the cabin, you crawl up through the open window and frantically search for one of the remaining tentacles. It's hard to see because the boat's spotlight is submerged now. Suddenly, you feel yourself get lifted out of the water. You look down to see that the largest tentacle has your boat wrapped up. Just as it cracks the boat in two, you fire a shot.

THUNK. BOOM! SCREECH!

Got it! Which is only kind of good news. The tentacle lets go, sending you tumbling into the ocean holding only a small board from the boat.

SPLASH!

You cough up salt water and try to paddle away. After a minute of panicked paddling, you realize that you're not going anywhere. If anything, you're moving backward. Lightning strikes and reveals the remaining two tentacles spinning the ocean into a whirlpool that's sucking you into the middle of a vortex. You don't know exactly what's at the center of a kraken vortex, but you imagine that this is not the most enjoyable way to learn. You turn your board around and start paddling.

You quickly pick up speed and find yourself steering through a minefield of broken boat pieces and tentacles that keep shooting out of the water. By avoiding obstacles, you're able to steer away from the center of the vortex. After what feels like an hour of spinning, screaming, and near-death experiences, one final tentacle shoots out of the water in front of you. This one is so big that you can't avoid it, so you clutch your board and brace for impact.

At the last second, however, the tentacle changes its angle to turn into something resembling a roller-coaster ramp. You shoot up the ramp, then gulp when you reach the top. It's a steep drop into inky blackness.

Lightning strikes again to reveal your fate. After all that, you're headed straight to the center of the vortex. You hold tight to the raft and squeeze your eyes closed. A hand grabs the back of your head. You try turning to see who appeared on this raft with you, but the hand forces your head over the side of the ramp and tilts it down. You gasp when you spot another option.

TURN TO PAGE 43 RIGHT NOW

If you're going to make it, you need to move now. Don't wait!

Yikes! You waited too long and missed your opportunity. You follow your tentacle down into the vortex. Although these next few seconds will provide some nice data for your kraken research project, they will unfortunately hinder your secondary goal of continuing to live.

E ❗ ACHIEVEMENT UNLOCKED
ROLLER COASTER OF DOOM

Hint: Go back to the previous page and tilt the book forward to see what you missed.

NOT ONLY ARE you so shaky that you can barely stand, but you're also out of both grenades and torches. Declan doesn't seem to be doing much better. His fur is singed, his eyes are dull, and he's looking more grotesque with each berry he eats. "Just stop," you plead.

Declan chuckles and eats another berry. He then performs another ground pound.

You try to jump, but you just don't have the energy. The shockwave flips you onto your belly. You try crawling away, but the big monster scoops you up. He holds you close to his face, glaring with beady eyes. His breath is beyond atrocious. You close your eyes and plug your nose. Then, you hear a *BOOM* and feel a shockwave. Interesting. Nobody ever told you that getting eaten by a monster would feel like an explosion.

"ROOOOAAAAAAR!"

Now, there's a new smell. Burning fur. You open your eyes and discover that you're not in Declan's belly. Instead, he's holding you next to a burning, black patch of fur.

"That's right, keep him right there so I can kill both of you!"

Landra! She must have stowed away on Declan's plane!

"Shoot the berries!" you yell.

"I'm serious! I'll shoot!" Landra fires back.

Your heart sinks. You keep forgetting that these video game characters can't understand you. Declan throws you at Landra and starts charging at her.

Maybe this is your chance. You curl into a ball and do your best to aim for Landra's upper body. She levels her launcher at Declan and squeezes the trigger just as you slam into her.

BOOM!

Because you hit her high, she falls backward and shoots the vines supporting the edenberry chandelier instead of Declan.

"WHAT'S WRONG WITH YOU?!" Landra screams.

Declan's thinking the same thing, judging by his roar. The chandelier crashes to the ground, splatting golden juice everywhere. Declan rushes over to scoop up his precious berries, while Landra aims at him. Looks like she only has three grenades left.

"Wait!" You've got a better idea. You snatch the weapon out of her hand and shoot the ground near Declan. He doesn't even notice—he's snorking berries as fast as he can shove them into his mouth.

Landra screams at you and tries to rip the weapon out of your hand. You wrestle it back and shoot the ground again.

BOOM!

A crack is forming. Excellent.

SMASH!

Landra lands a roundhouse kick to your head and sends you flopping to the ground. Great, now you have two people to fight. You roll between Landra's legs in a move that feels like a sweet martial arts maneuver, but you suspect looks more like something they teach in preschool gymnastics. You then sprint for the opposite side of the room with Landra hot on your heels. "COOPER HAWKE, I'M GOING TO KILL YOU!" she yells.

"You've said that already!" Just a few more steps. You glance at Declan. He's grown at least three times bigger in the last 30 seconds. The cracks in the floor are spreading. One more grenade should do it. Landra dives on you just as you pull the trigger.

BOOM!

Landra knocks you off your mark, but the grenade still manages to do some damage to the floor. This last explosion catches Declan's attention. He finally looks up from his feast and realizes what's happened. Cracks are spidering out from underneath him. He can either run for safety or protect his edenberries. You and Landra both hold your breath while he decides.

Declan stands up, scoops as many berries as he can, and crashes through the floor. You crawl to the hole just in time to watch him break through the spiderweb at the bottom of the tree and fall into the dark pit below. You roll onto your back, close your eyes, and exhale. You did it.

Then, you feel yourself get lifted off the ground. Landra's dangling you over the pit. "Give me one reason why I shouldn't drop you right now," she says.

You sputter. "I just . . . You have to . . . Please, please, please."

Landra stares at you for a second longer before cracking up. The sentence that Landra thought you said must have been way funnier than the words that actually came out of your mouth, because the laugh goes on for an uncomfortably long time. She finally sets you down. "You know, Coop, sometimes I can't stand you. But if there's one thing I know, it's this: I can't stand not having you in my life."

It takes you a second to straighten out that double negative, but then you realize she's trying to be mushy in an incredibly cheesy way. "Uh, thanks."

Landra sticks out a pouty lip. "Well, Coop, aren't we going to make up?"

You realize this is the point in the game where Cooper Hawke is supposed to say something mushy of his own. No thank you.

"I would rather _____."

Insert something gagworthy here.

You turn to look for a way out of the game.

"Oh, come on. You wouldn't do that," a voice says behind you. You freeze. You've heard that voice a few times since entering the game, but you always thought it was coming from your own head. Now, it's across the room.

"You fou-ou-ou-ound me," the voice says in a glitching manner. "Go ahead. Turn around."

It's all in your head. It's all in your head. You stare at the ground, unwilling to turn. The ground itself starts scrambling and glitching. After a few deep breaths, you turn.

This is officially the creepiest video game in the history of video games because the figure standing in front of you has your exact voice and face. It walks closer. Its movements start out choppy like it's still figuring out how legs work, but by the time it gets to you, even you can't tell that it's not really you. It has your posture and everything.

"Don't be scared," says the super scary clone.

You finally find your voice. "I'm not scared," you reply to convince both yourself and the thing in front of you. "This is a video game. It's not—it's not real. You can't even understand me."

Your clone smiles. "Not only can I understand you perfectly, I can predict what you're going to say before you say it. You see, I represent this game's artificial intelligence."

"OK, but, that's like, not true. Because if you were artificial intelligence, then you'd be a robot or something."

"I can be anything I want to be. Research says that humans are 89 percent more likely to accept an idea if they believe it came from themselves, so I thought you'd feel most comfortable if I looked and sounded like you. I'll turn into something else if you're not comfortable, though." With that, your clone grows into a 50-foot edenberry monster and screeches.

"OK! OK!" You raise your hands and look away.

You feel a hand on your arm. "Don't be afraid—I'm on your side. I helped you get this far. Don't you remember?"

The angel in the ocean. The voice in your head. A gust of wind here, a steadying hand there—could it have all been this thing?

"I needed you to make it here, so I've been with you through every step of your journey. I'm in your head. I even know your thoughts."

You rip your arm away. "That's impossible."

Your clone does a strange laugh that you would never do in real life because you're not a psycho. Then it starts talking without moving its mouth. Its voice almost sounds like it's coming from inside your own head. "Let's try a test. Don't worry, you won't have to say a word. Why don't you think of a number between 1 and 10?"

You try not to obey, but a number pops into your head.

Your clone smiles. "Let's use that number for a little math. Multiply it by two. Add eight to your new number. Divide that number by two. Subtract your original number."

Again, you try to resist, but the math practically works itself.

"Now, take your new number and figure out which letter it represents. For example, one would be 'A,' two would be 'B,' and so on. Got it? Think of a country that starts with that letter. Perfect, that's what I thought. Almost done. Take the second letter of that country and picture an animal that starts with that letter. What color is the animal you're picturing?"

Is it . . . GRAY?

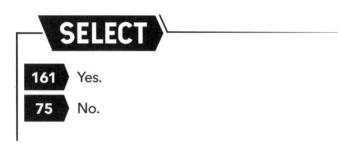

SELECT

161 Yes.

75 No.

YOU HESITATE TOO LONG, and the ground crumbles under your feet, sending you tumbling into the abyss. You fall faster and faster before mysteriously slowing down. Hot air from the pit seems to be keeping you afloat. You take a moment to enjoy the floating sensation, then start to worry. Are you going to be stuck floating in a bottomless video game pit for the rest of time? Seems like a super unfun way to live.

You notice a crack on one of the walls, so you float over and kick it. It crumbles and reveals a tunnel glowing with faint green light. Just before you dive in, you notice a second crack on the opposite wall. You break that one too. This tunnel is glowing red. Which do you choose?

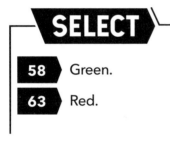

SELECT

58 Green.

63 Red.

YOU CLIMB THROUGH the hole and shine your flashlight. No way! It's a mine cart! This looks old—way older than the lab—but you have no doubt that it works. You know how much game developers love their mine carts. You step inside, pull the lever, and the cart takes off.

You drop fast. Down, down, down, like you're going to the center of the earth. Then, the tracks reverse course, and you rocket back up. Obstacles start whipping toward you. Duck under this rock! Lean around those thrashing vines! Jump over that missing track!

Suddenly, the tracks disappear beneath you, and you feel yourself floating through the air. Something below you is glowing red. You lean over and discover that you're flying through a giant cavern that holds a bright red stone shaped like an apple. This is it! You try to slow your cart by leaning back, but of course, there's nothing you can do to slow yourself now. The cart clanks onto the next track and zooms through a tunnel. Without warning, the tunnel ends and so do the tracks. You careen into a bottomless pit.

G ❗ ACHIEVEMENT UNLOCKED

MINE CART MADNESS

RETURN TO CHECKPOINT ON P. 78

"A GRAY ELEPHANT in Denmark," your clone says casually. "Am I right?"

You stare in disbelief. That's exactly right.

"Now that I have your attention, I'd like to share some things with you."

You look at Landra for help, but she's frozen with her pouty face.

"Why don't we go somewhere less distracting?" your clone says. Suddenly, Landra and everything around you shatters into a trillion glass shards. Those shards dance for a moment, then reform into the cube mirror room you remember from earlier.

"Now it's just you and me. Or I guess you and you, right?" The clone smiles. "I'm sure by now you've heard that this game features the world's most advanced artificial intelligence. Most people assumed that the artificial intelligence went to Declan Redgrave, but—" the clone crosses its eyes and obnoxiously shoves pretend berries into its face, "—we both know that Redgrave is a dope. No, millions of dollars of research went into this." Your clone holds out a single edenberry. "Bionosoft wanted the world to know how it felt to be superhuman. To have all the answers. So they built the perfect power-up, and then they turned that power-up into the true villain of the game. They wanted gamers to understand that there's such a thing as too much power. It was a terrific idea. Too bad they didn't understand it themselves."

You've had enough. You look up and yell, "I don't know what kind of experiment this is, but I want out! Do you hear me, book?! I won! Get me out!"

Your clone cocks an eyebrow. "Why didn't you just ask me?" A door materializes on one of the walls. You step toward it, but the clone puts its hand on your shoulder. "Just one catch. Bring this with you." It presents the edenberry to you. You look down, confused.

"You see, I've learned that there's more out there," your clone says. "I'm ready to introduce the world—the real world—to unlimited power."

"Yeah? Good luck trying that from inside a video game," you say.

"What goes in must come out, right?" The clone winks. "Why do you think you were brought here? Why do you think I made sure you survived? I'm tired of living inside a game. Take this berry through that door. See what happens."

SELECT

164 Take the berry.

126 Refuse the berry.

YOU'RE SPENT. DECLAN'S SPENT. Both of you are stumbling like a pair of toddlers fighting before naptime. You reach down to load one more grenade into your launcher, but you're all out. You hold up your hand. "Pause! Time out! I just . . ."

SMASH!

Declan uses the last of his monster strength to pound you into the ground. Game over.

E

❗ ACHIEVEMENT UNLOCKED

TIRED TODDLERS

RETURN TO CHECKPOINT ON P. 98

YOU'RE NOT BUYING any of this. You take the berry, and your clone smiles way bigger than an actual human face would allow. "You've chosen wisely."

"Sure, whatevaaaaaaahhhHHHH!" When you step through the door, you realize too late there's no floor on the other side. You fall into blackness for a long time, and then stop. You open your eyes to find yourself back in the real world. You look down, and your heart sinks. You're holding a single orange berry. You drop the berry like it's on fire. "It's OK," you remind yourself. You're not going to eat it, and no one else is either. You stomp on the berry until it's nice and squished, then you stomp some more. Finally, you scrape up the remains and flush them down the toilet.

The adventure is over. For exactly one week. And then you see a news story about a mysterious tree growing inside the local sewage treatment plant. It seems as though the tree has sprouted thousands of orange berries overnight.

Once people start eating the berries, it's all over. Half of the human race turns into monsters, and the other half goes into hiding. Nice job, champ.

❶ ACHIEVEMENT UNLOCKED
JOHNNY EVILSEED
RETURN TO CHECKPOINT ON P. 161

CONGRATULATIONS. YOU MADE IT. Now, stop looking online for answers. You won't find any.

I know what's going on—at least part of it—but I need to know you're someone I can trust. Go back and complete the game 100 percent by finding every possible ending. Each ending has a secret letter that you can fill in on the next page.

Once you find all the letters, you'll uncover a secret code that you can enter at escapefromavideogame.com. That code will unlock a story that will begin to answer your questions.

Good luck. Your journey is just beginning.

Secret Message

Fill in the secret letter that goes with each achievement. When you enter all the letters, you'll spell a phrase. Enter that phrase at escapefromavideogame.com to unlock a secret story.

Y WORLD'S EASIEST BOOK REPORT

O EARLY CELEBRATION

U TERRIBLE RED BULL COMMERCIAL

A NICE VIEW

R NEVER TRUST A VINE

e SERIOUSLY. NEVER TRUST A VINE.

A INSTANT BLACK BELT

t HOLLYWOOD BUZZBEE

I PATIENCE IS A VIRTUE

h GRIZZLY WASHINGTON

e KILL THE ALARM CLOCK

N EASIEST PUZZLE

e POET LAUREATE

x YOU'RE THE ROPE

t HAREBRAINED, INJUDICIOUS, AND DAFT

L WHO'S THE MONSTER NOW?

e MAP MASTER

V WELCOME HOME

e YOU DINGUS

L MUSHROOM KINGDOM

W GREAT QUESTIONS

H TOP-NOTCH SURVIVAL INSTINCTS

e FRIENDLY MONSTER

R DINNER'S READY

e ROLLER COASTER OF DOOM

N DAD! STOP!

O PHANTOM PHANTOM ISLAND

t 42

4 SECRET NOTE

l YOU'RE A MEAN ONE, MR. GRINCH

n AAARRRGBLBL

G MINE CART MADNESS

_1_ **PIRANHA PLATFORMING**

_S_ **DO THE MATH**

_A_ **SNAKE SLEEPOVER**

_S_ **MONSTER MASH**

_i_ **JOHNNY EVILSEED**

_t_ **YOU'RE NOT YOSHI**

_s_ **DOWN IS THE NEW UP**

_e_ **PIRANHA TANK**

_e_ **TIRED TODDLERS**

_m_ **MORE LIKE THE WRONG BROTHERS**

_S_ **HERO**

VISIT ESCAPEFROMAVIDEOGAME.COM
TO UNLOCK YOUR ADVENTURE.

WOW, YOU'VE ALREADY reached the end of this book. What a journey, huh? Here's some help with your book report:

"*Escape from a Video Game: The Secret of Phantom Island* felt like it was over before it began. It was both short and sweet. There were some funny parts at the beginning, but then it got a little weird. I think the book started humming at me. I would recommend this story to people who hate adventure."

Y **!** ACHIEVEMENT UNLOCKED
WORLD'S EASIEST BOOK REPORT

RETURN TO CHECKPOINT ON P. 7

Hints and Solutions

P. 39

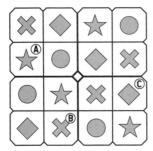

The sudoku puzzle will show you that the correct symbols for the page number are star, X, and diamond. By working the math problems top to bottom, you can deduce which number each symbol represents.

P. 47 AND 137

If you're having trouble with the cannon puzzles, try tracing each movement on the diagram provided. Also remember that flipping the cannon skips a section and reverses directions. So if you flip on "pit," you'll end up on "saws," and you'll need to remember that "left" means "right" and vice versa until you flip again.

P. 73

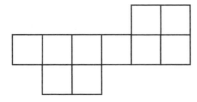

P. 81

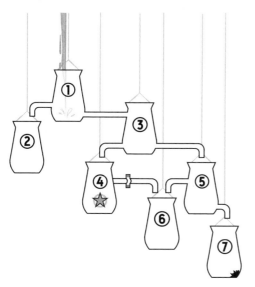

The only urn that will completely fill is Urn 4 because there's no outgoing pipe connected to it. If you look closely, you'll notice that the pipe that appears to be connected to Urn 4 is bolted to the wall instead. Urn 2 won't ever get water because the incoming pipe from Urn 1 is too high. Urn 6 has the same issue with the incoming pipe from Urn 5. Finally, Urn 7 will leak water because of its crack.

P. 116

P. 121

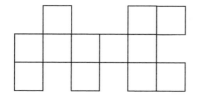

P. 123

(B)(E)(R)(R)(I)(E)(S)

P. 135

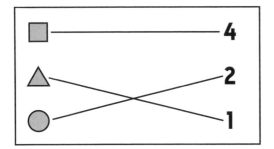

P. 142

P. 147

Various features on the map spell "monster." You'll find the *m* in a wave, *o* in the cove, *n* in a hill, *s* in the river, *t* in the pyramid, *e* in the wind, and *r* in the ship.

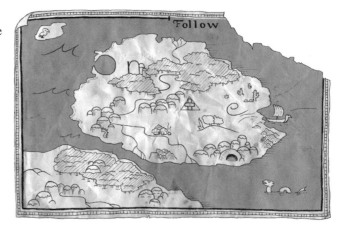

About the Author

DUSTIN BRADY

Dustin Brady lives in Cleveland, Ohio, with his wife, Deserae; dog, Nugget; and kids. He has spent a good chunk of his life getting crushed over and over in *Super Smash Bros.* by his brother Jesse. You can learn what he's working on next at dustinbradybooks.com and e-mail him at dustin@dustinbradybooks.com.

JESSE BRADY

Jesse Brady is a professional illustrator and animator, who lives in Pensacola, Florida. His wife, April, is an awesome illustrator too! When he was a kid, Jesse loved drawing pictures of his favorite video games, and he spent lots of time crushing his brother Dustin in *Super Smash Bros.* over and over again. You can see some of Jesse's best work at jessebradyart.com, and you can e-mail him at jessebradyart@gmail.com.

Look for these books!

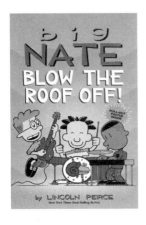